To Googie and John, with love

I have been studying how I may compare
This prison where I live unto the world;
And for because the world is populous,
And here is not a creature but myself,
I cannot do it – yet I'll hammer it out.

Shakespeare, Richard II

PART ONE

Obsession

CHAPTER ONE

She saw Bruce at the far end of the corridor, and stretched out her arms to him, calling to him urgently. He didn't seem to hear her and retreated backwards down the ever-lengthening passage, faster and faster until she could hardly make him out. It was dark, but he appeared to be lit by a nimbus of light. She felt helpless as he dwindled, helpless and desperate. She knew she should have run to him, but she was scared, scared of her own inadequacy. If he had wanted her, he would have stayed with her. But he had gone ...

June awoke, sweating with fear. She lay in bed shaking, reliving the horror, then, with an effort, turned on the bedside lamp to look at the clock. It was morning: time, if she wanted, to pull back the heavily lined silk curtains, and start the new day. Sunlight flooded into the room, hurting her eyes. She went to the bedroom door, brought in the Sunday papers from the floor outside, then settled herself down among the pillows to read; but she found it hard to concentrate.

She had had a matinée and evening show the day before, so had arranged nothing for today; she would be able to indulge herself in a long lie-in. Bruce, her husband, was evidently already at his desk in his study next door; probably working on the new play he was due to hand in for production in three weeks' time. She could hear the jerky clatter of his typewriter. Since by now he was a successful playwright, the play had already been accepted; it would go into rehearsal at the end of the month then, after a longish prior-to-London tour,

3

would open in London in a theatre which had already been booked.

The telephone bell shrilled, and June picked up the receiver by her bed. The caller was Mary Goodson – Philip's wife. She sounded strained, but composed. She spoke steadily and without emphasis, but in a clipped, high, clear voice.

'I'm sorry to bother you, but I am ringing you to ask you a favour.'

'Yes?' asked June, and she felt her heart sink.

'I wondered if you would come and visit me some time fairly soon. I know you're in a play in the West End just now, and I know Suffolk is rather a bore to get to, but we could give you a bed for the night – it would have to be a Sunday, wouldn't it? You see – I'm afraid I've got cancer, and they don't give me very long.'

'How awful!' exclaimed June, shocked. 'I'm so very sorry.'

'Yes, well I've more or less come to terms with it now.' Mary hurried on. 'The visit needn't be tomorrow, if you see what I mean, but I'd feel easier in my mind if I could have a word with you.'

'Of course I'll come,' said June. Her mind teemed with questions it would be impossible to ask. 'How is Philip?'

'If you mean does he know I'm ringing you, yes he does, and he's looking forward to seeing you. He's taken all this rather badly I'm afraid, and that's being one of the most difficult things. Neither of us has "known the worst", as they say, for all that long, and he hasn't had time to get himself adjusted. I'm not in much pain yet, and have plenty of pills so I don't feel too bad.'

'Could you give me any idea what you want to talk about?'

'No, I don't think I can. Not over the phone. Any weekend will suit us.'

'The only trouble is that we're giving a big party for Pippa's twenty-first birthday in a few weeks' time, and I'm in

4

charge of the arrangements as Bruce's new play is starting rehearsal soon.'

'I understand.'

'May I get the diary?'

'Please.'

'One minute.'

June fetched the diary, and after comparing dates the two women arranged for a weekend eight weeks ahead.

'That's not too far away?' asked June uncomfortably. 'I'll try to put something off if you'd rather?'

'No. Please don't.'

'Right. See you then.'

'Thank you. Goodbye.'

June put down the receiver.

Bruce wouldn't like her going to Suffolk. He had never forgiven her for going back to Philip after their marriage; had never really trusted her since.

He walked into the room at that moment, and she saw his anger immediately. His thick grey hair was rumpled, and the silk dressing gown he wore over his shirt was creased, but he still looked elegant and impressive. A solid handsome man, blue-eyed, broad-faced and powerful. Her husband.

'What was all that about?' he asked.

'Mary Goodson,' June replied.

'I gathered that much before I put down the receiver,' he said. 'What does she want?'

'She's dying of cancer, and wants me to go to Suffolk one weekend,' said June.

'Good God! Why on earth? You haven't seen either of them for years, have you?'

'No. But she wants to talk to me.'

'What about?'

'Philip, I presume.'

'I don't like the sound of it,' said Bruce. 'Sounds a bit mawkish. I hope you refused?'

'I couldn't. How could I?'

'What good can it do?'

'There seems to be something on her mind,' said June, unhappily. He frowned. 'After all. I suppose I owe it to her. I did try to get Philip away from her for years. Surely it's the least I can do?'

'Can't you ever let the business rest?' demanded Bruce sourly. 'That affair of yours with Philip has bedevilled all our lives. It bedevilled yours for a decade before we married, and it must have bedevilled theirs.'

'It wasn't I who rang. Mary rang me,' protested June. 'She wants me to go, and apparently Philip does too.'

'You certainly don't owe Philip anything,' said Bruce, emphatically. 'The man's a pain.' He paused, then continued: 'Are you sure it's for her sake? You're not still carrying a torch for him?'

'Of course not! You know I'm not!'

'Do I?' asked Bruce. 'Love can be very persistent.'

Yes indeed, thought June. Aloud she said, 'I have no feeling at all for him.' But even as she spoke she knew she was lying. 'If Mary wasn't dying, nothing on God's earth would get me to go there.'

'Supposing I asked you not to?'

'I've already accepted. Besides why should you mind? You know I love you – you and Pippa are the most important people in my life.'

'I dislike the idea.'

'I can't let her down now.'

'OK.' He made a small but definite expression of disapproval and left the room.

How complicated life was. Bruce was rapidly becoming a stranger, and yet once they'd been so happy together! She sighed. He'd been sleeping around for some time now and she knew that her affair with Philip had started it. But she hadn't seen Philip for five years – and what she had just said, about

6

Bruce and Pippa being the two most important people in her life, was true. To have Bruce back as the adoring husband he had once been would give her more happiness than anything else she could think of. But their relationship was spiralling downwards into a void. And things were no better with her daughter.

Pippa had always idolised her father; but lately in June's eyes this emotion had become unhealthy. At one time she had thought that she shared some of her daughter's love. Now she believed she had none. Right from the time she was a baby, the sun had risen and set for Pippa on Bruce, and Bruce, knowing that he came a poor second to Philip in June's affections, had encouraged her preference. So, out of a sense of guilt, had June, pleased that Bruce had at least one of the family to care for him with such passion. Now the situation had got out of hand. Pippa's jealousy at any signs of reconciliation between her parents was persistent and malicious. Another 'reward' for the affair with Philip?

Perhaps Pippa would find more demanding work soon, and things would improve. The series of jobs she had taken after leaving school, culminating in the 'help' she was giving in her friend's antique shop, hadn't really taxed her intelligence. She was a clever girl, and needed to use her brain. She was also devastatingly beautiful, so perhaps she would soon marry and leave home.

June sighed again and lay back against the pillows.

She was a pretty fair-haired woman in her forties. Her face was as yet unlined, and she still had a superb figure. Not a sign yet of the sudden onset of fat which afflicts so many women of her age. She had a beautiful skin, grey eyes and a deep, rather husky voice. She moved well and had a natural elegance. She was also a good actress. But her besetting sin was a too vivid desire to please, combined with too little faith in herself. This had led to trouble all her life, and would, she was sure, continue to do so.

She closed her eyes, and her thoughts returned to the early days of her affair with Philip.

Because of that affair so much of her life had been lived on two levels – the successful actress, charming, intelligent, coping with marriage, a child and a career; and the unhappy, desperate prisoner, endlessly trying to escape a relentless love ...

CHAPTER TWO

June was eighteen, and in her second term at drama school. Philip was a good-looking young actor on the staff. He was also working in a play in the West End, which gave him great glamour in the eyes of most of the pupils. (In those days, before the National and the Royal Shakespeare Company, the West End was considered the height of a theatre actor's ambition.) He was thirty-five and married to a loving and complaisant wife, whom he in his turn loved in his own fashion; but the conquest of other women was a necessity to him. As he valued his relationship with his wife too highly ever to become closely involved with the girls he seduced, there were many unpleasant scenes and much unhappiness. Most of the girls at the school fancied they were in love with him, and June, shy, susceptible and completely inexperienced, joined their number. Unfortunately for her, Philip was equally strongly attracted.

She had hardly seen him during her first term as she was in none of his classes, but he directed one of the plays she was in during the following term, and she was thrown often into his company in that most titillating of situations for many women: pupil and master.

She recognised intuitively the insecurity in him, which made her sorry for him; but it was also an added attraction. She shrewdly guessed that he wouldn't have been teaching drama students if he had confidence in his ability as an actor. In turn, Philip recognised her inexperience, her gentleness

9

and her evident sincerity. He also admired her talent, obvious even at this stage.

June had lived all her life in the country, before passing her audition for the school. Her father, the Rev. Henry Mansfield, was vicar of a small parish in Dorset; her mother, Josie, was a plump, mousy, over-anxious little woman who muddled her way through a life filled with domesticity and good works, loving her vague handsome husband, but understanding little of what he was saying, as he was academically inclined. The house was untidy and badly run, and the food was deplorable (especially during the war, when shortages lowered the standard even further); but June was devoted to them both.

The war had started when June was eight; by 1941, she already knew that she wanted to be an actress. In bed with measles during the school holidays, she had read on two consecutive days *The Hound of the Baskervilles* and *The Merchant of Venice*. From then on she read all the Sherlock Holmes books she could lay her hands on, and kept one or other of the Shakespeare plays by her bed. The difficulty of Shakespeare's language, far from putting her off, increased the mystery and fascination of the plays for her, and soon in her mind's eye she became Portia, Rosalind, Viola and Desdemona. When she went back to school she asked to be enrolled in the drama class, and it was discovered that she had a real talent for acting.

Both parents were alarmed at such a turn of affairs. The theatre had never entered their heads as an idea for a career for her. Neither of them were theatre-goers: to both of them the word 'actress' was a synonym for 'fast' and 'hard', 'sophisticated' and 'ostentatious'. During the war years, there seemed no chance of June getting her way; but peace came when she was fourteen, and from then on she was absolutely determined to go into the theatre. Although she had never before set herself against them, at seventeen

10

she at last persuaded her parents to let her have a try.

To everyone's surprise but her own, she passed the audition for the Warren Davies School of Drama in Earl's Court, found herself a room on the top floor of a lodging house in Fulham, and at once settled down to make a new life. She found it difficult at first to make friends with the other students in the house, because she felt herself to be such a country bumpkin, but there were many others equally unused to London, and even at this stage her talent gave her their respect.

She enjoyed everything at the school uncritically, except for the fencing classes for which she had no aptitude. In any case the fencing instructor was a bully. Fortunately she found the dancing, exercises to music, voice lessons, radio lessons, make-up classes and stage training exhilarating, and above all there were the plays to be rehearsed.

She went home after the first term so obviously happy that her parents' fears were more or less stilled. She was no more sophisticated, and certainly hadn't become hard or ostentatious. She was pleased to see her mother and father, but the holidays seemed to drag, and she returned to London three days early with vague excuses of 'preparatory work'.

By the end of her very first class with Philip she was attracted, and within a few weeks she was hopelessly in love. The play he was directing her in was *Still Life* by Noël Coward (which had become the famous film, *Brief Encounter*), and soon she was imagining herself and Philip to be the two sad people whose love for each other could never be consummated as both were married to people they liked.

She had discovered that Philip was married from a chance remark made on the first day. Then it hadn't mattered to her. Very soon it did. Because of Philip's attraction she hardly noticed the boy with whom she was acting and, sensing her infatuation, Philip kept her back after lessons to have 'extra

11

study on her technique'. He asked her if she had ever been kissed, and she said 'No', because she had never really been attracted before. He asked her if she had ever been in love, and she said 'No'. He was charmed by her blushes and obvious adoration, and he told her that someone must teach her how to make love on stage. He suggested that he could show her himself, if she thought it a good idea. Naturally she agreed. When he kissed her she felt faint, and he noticed his effect with pleasure.

From then on Philip kept her guessing as to when he would give her such lessons; playing her warily, like a cat with a bird. His kisses became more and more passionate, but as they were supposed to be lessons, he had a complete mastery of the situation. Utterly besotted, June was alternately in a state of ecstasy or misery. Philip enjoyed it all immensely.

After the 'love-making' June tried to get him to talk about himself, but he evidently didn't like this. She wanted to know about his real feelings for her, naturally, but he shied away from the subject, although leading her to believe he might care. She wanted to know about his feelings for his wife, too, but again he refused to be drawn. Indeed, when not involved in these curious classes he was often off-hand and almost brusque with her. She began sleeping badly, and her other lessons began to suffer. She tried to pull herself together, but it was first love: an emotion more intense than anything she had even distantly imagined. Her rehearsals of *Still Life*, however, showed a growing mastery of feeling and technique, and after the public show at the end of term she received great praise.

The second holidays were almost upon her. There was an eight-week break during the summer months, and she was in despair because she wouldn't be seeing him again for so long.

On the last day of school, while she was packing, Philip found her in the main classroom and called her to his office.

12

She followed him anxiously. He told her to sit down and wait while he finished some paperwork and she sat uncomfortably on the wooden chair opposite his desk, gazing at him while he wrote out reports. He was certainly good to look at. She noticed the thickness of his brown hair, and the way it curled round his small ears. She noticed the smoothness of his tanned skin, the fairness of his eyebrows, the sensuality of his mouth, and the rather heavy jowls. She noticed how beautiful his hands were and how well they were manicured, and she could faintly smell the expensive after-shave he always wore. From time to time he raised his head from his writing and gazed into space, and she gazed back at him mesmerised. Once, he seemed to become aware of her, and smiled. Her mouth went dry, and her heart seemed to turn over. She mocked herself for being so love-sick, but love-sick she was, and there seemed to be nothing she could do about it.

At long last he put down his pen, and looked directly at her. It was a long steady stare, and she blushed ferociously.

'Come here, June,' he said softly. 'Here, close to me. Now, look at me. Have you enjoyed working with me?'

'You know I have.'

'Very much?'

'Oh, yes.'

'There is some talk we shall do so again next term. Would you like that?'

'It would be wonderful!'

'The trouble is that we don't really know each other yet, do we?'

'Don't we?'

He affected surprise. 'Do you think you know me?'

'No. No. Of course not, but I thought you must know me. There's so little to know.'

'Silly girl,' he said softly. 'Would you like us to get to know each other better?'

'Yes.' She was pathetically eager.

13

'Have you any appointments to keep at the moment?'

'No. I was just packing, as you saw.'

'Give me your hand.'

She held it out, and he took it, stroking the back of it insistently; then he jerked her towards him, and put his arms round her waist, looking up at her. 'Do you think you'll forget those lessons in kissing?' he asked.

'Of course not.'

'You enjoyed them?'

'Yes.' She could hardly speak.

He grinned and stood up. 'Well, then,' he said, 'we'll go a little further in your education. Would you like that?'

'I – I think so.'

He sounded impatient. 'Would you or wouldn't you?' he asked.

'Yes.'

'Right.' He locked the door. 'Undo your blouse.'

Clumsily she did as she was told.

'Now your bra.'

'Must I?'

'Just take off the damned thing and let me have a look at you!'

He stared at her breasts, cupped one of them in his hand, seemed to think deeply for a moment, then said, 'Yes. You'll do. Take everything off. And hurry – we haven't got all the time in the world.'

Bewildered, she undressed, then he pushed her back on to the small divan in the corner of the room. He took off his jacket, his trousers and his pants, and seduced her quickly and expertly, and through the chaos of her emotions – shock, elation, fright and passion – her predominant feeling was one of triumphant happiness.

'Foolish little virgin!' he said, and laughed. 'You'd better get out of here fast.'

'Now?' she asked, surprised.

14

'Now,' he said.

'But when shall I see you again?' she asked, and suddenly she felt tears pricking her eyes.

'Do you want to?'

'Yes.'

He considered this for a moment while pulling on his trousers. 'What are you doing tonight?'

'Nothing.'

'Right. Get in some food and wine at your place – here's a fiver – and I'll be round at about seven. Write down the address for me.'

She did so. And from that day onwards she was hooked.

He came to her that evening (his play had closed a fortnight previously) and he put himself out to charm, complimenting her on her looks, on the way she had tried to brighten up her little room, on her cooking, and on her acting. He made her talk about herself, and listened with interest to all she had to say, but as usual he told her little about himself. She asked him if he was happy with his wife, and he said he'd never leave her but that marriage was an unnatural state for anyone.

'For your wife?' she interrupted quickly.

He looked surprised. 'No. I don't suppose it is. She's a real home-maker, which is probably why she makes a good wife.'

June found this far from encouraging. She struggled with herself for a moment, then said, 'Do you still sleep with her?'

'What's that got to do with anything?' he asked, and he sounded slightly aggressive.

'Nothing. Nothing at all,' she replied hastily.

'Well if you really want to know, I do,' he said. 'Why not? She'd be unhappy if I didn't.'

June found this reply confusing.

Philip went on. 'Sleeping with people is a much over-rated pastime. I can't say I don't enjoy it enormously, but it's not

15

be-all and end-all of a marriage. Which is why marriage is different from an affair.'

'Is your wife pretty?'

'Not as pretty as you,' he said, smiling at her fondly. 'But then she's a lot older. After all, I'm very nearly twice your age.'

'And she?'

'Thirty-one or thirty-two. I'm hopeless at remembering such things.' He looked at his watch. 'Heavens!' he exclaimed. 'I'll have to go quite soon. Let's go to bed. It's better in bed, and it will be better still soon when you've stopped being a frightened little virgin, and I've taught you a thing or two.'

'Are you disappointed in me?'

'You talk too much. Hurry.'

Before he left her he said, 'Tomorrow, same time same place. Will that suit you?'

'Oh, yes.'

'Oh, yes,' he repeated, and laughed. 'One day you'll have to grow up, won't you?'

After he'd gone she rang her parents to say she'd been unavoidably delayed in coming down to them, then crept back into bed and tried to recapture the evening, moment by moment.

CHAPTER THREE

For a week Philip made love to her every night, and the world
became a magical place for her. She tried to dismiss all
disquieting thoughts, and to enjoy only the marvellous realis-
ation that she was passionately in love. She walked round in a
daze, shopping and cooking in a trance of love; and as a lover
she tried to be a brilliant pupil. She still couldn't make out
Philip's actual feelings for her. He often called her foolish, but
then he called her clever, too. She knew that he wouldn't
return to her so often if he had found her unsatisfactory, but
she still couldn't get him to talk about himself, except in the
most general terms, or – very occasionally – about the other
women to whom he had made love.

'Have you ever *been* in love?' she asked.

'Yes.'

'With your wife?'

'Love is a disease,' he said. 'It's the worst disease there is.'

'I think it's wonderful.'

He grinned. 'You don't know anything,' he said. 'You're
the youngest person for your age I've ever met.'

'D'you mind?'

'It amuses me.'

'Have you loved lots of women?'

'Millions.'

'No, seriously.'

'Seriously, yes, a great many, but I really haven't counted!'

'Have you hurt any of them?'

17

For a moment he looked very angry indeed, then he said quietly, 'Perhaps.'

'Don't you mind?'

'Some women beg to be hurt.' He seemed to shy away from the word *hurt*, and his eyes blazed furiously.

'Have *you* been hurt?'

'I told you, love's a disease. One should take sex casually.'

'I can't. Love is so tremendous.'

'I said sex.'

'Do you love me?'

'Chatter! Chatter! Chatter!' he exclaimed, smiling at her stiffly and ruffling her hair.

'Because if I didn't love you I couldn't deceive your wife.'

'I see.'

'Don't you mind deceiving your wife for casual sex?'

'It would be far worse for her if I actually loved someone else, wouldn't it?'

'Would it?'

'Of course.'

'Then you don't love me?'

'Relax, darling. Stop asking these endless questions. If you're having a good time with me, thank your lucky stars for the fun you're having. Count your blessings!'

'That makes no sense to me.'

He drew away from her and sat up in the bed. 'Look,' he said, 'if all this worries you so much, we'll skip it. I've enjoyed it. I'm sorry it hasn't satisfied you.'

'Oh, but it has.'

He looked at the watch he always wore. 'Time to go,' he said, 'and my wife will be back at the weekend, so I can't come to you again. You'd better be off to those creepy parents of yours, hadn't you? We'll see each other next term – OK?'

'But we can't not see each other until then! I shall die!'

'Rubbish.'

18

'I didn't mean to upset you, really I didn't!'

'You haven't upset me.'

'Couldn't you see me just once again?'

'No, darling. I'm sorry. Anyway, it will give you time to sort yourself out. Me, too. And we'll see what the future brings.'

'May I write to you?'

'Certainly not. No telephoning, either. I don't want my wife worried. She hasn't been very well, lately.'

'What's the matter with her?'

'A summer cold, and a bit of depression. She's been staying with one of her sisters, and the sister's got children and we haven't. It always sends her broody.'

'Don't you want children?'

'If she wants them, OK, but I can't say I mind for myself.' His face went suddenly blank.

He dressed rapidly, then kissed her and said, 'No moping, mind. We'll be seeing each other in seven weeks' time. That's not long.'

'It's the end of the world.'

He smiled. 'Have a lovely holiday. Keep well, and don't forget all I've taught you.'

She felt a lump come into her throat, and her face crumpled.

'Don't,' he said, sharply. 'I can't bear it. Women always cry, and they look awful when they cry. I don't want to remember you looking awful. Don't see me out,' he added. Then he left the room, and she heard him going fast down the stairs, and the slam of the front door.

When she reached home, June found to her dismay that her grandmother had come to stay.

Mrs Granger was as unlike Josie Mansfield as any mother could be. She was tall and slim with a long face, beautiful grey hair always immaculately in place, dark eyes, and

19

splendid white teeth. Her speech was precise and a little mannered. She was extremely clever and suffered no fools gladly, including her daughter. Unlike her daughter again, she was an agnostic.

'Just because I don't believe in God,' she would say, 'doesn't mean He doesn't exist. I take the very reasonable position that I simply don't know. No one can possibly know, and I haven't been blessed with faith – although I'm willing to admit that we need God psychologically as a bridge to our intimations of a spirit world.'

'Don't say things like that, Mother,' Josie would reply, piteously. 'It isn't right! It especially isn't right in this house! It also isn't fair on Henry. After all, it's his life's work to persuade people that God exists.'

'I can't be hypocritical,' said Mrs Granger firmly, 'and I should hope you wouldn't want me to.'

'You needn't talk about your beliefs at all when you're staying here,' protested Josie.

'I thought honesty was a virtue!' retorted Mrs Granger.

'Sometimes honesty can be hurtful.' Josie was near tears.

'My dear, you asked me to stay. What am I going to talk about if I can't say what I think?'

'I asked you to stay because I thought you might be lonely,' said Josie.

'Oh, very cheering!' replied her mother. 'I hoped it might be for your sake as much as mine.'

'Of course it is. You know it is! You always make things so difficult. You do it on purpose!' Mrs Granger laughed and Josie continued wildly, 'You've always teased me, and you know it makes me miserable.' Her lower lip began trembling.

'There, now,' said Mrs Granger pacifically. 'Don't cry.'

'I don't think you've ever really loved me,' sniffed Josie unhappily. She dabbed her reddened nose with a large handkerchief.

'Rubbish! I've loved you as much as I could ever love any

20

child, although I can't say I like children much. I didn't want children, but Richard did, and he always got his own way. I was in love with the wretched man for years.'

'What a way to talk about Father! He's dead ...'

'Do you think I don't know it?' Mrs Granger suddenly looked desperate. 'You can't imagine how hateful it is to be a widow. Better Richard than no one. You're right that I'm lonely, so of course it was nice of you to have me here, and I'm sorry I snapped at you.' Josie smiled a watery smile and Mrs Granger went on quickly, 'There are so many widows that you join a gloomy sort of club when your man dies. Non-members don't give you much sympathy after the funeral is over. Most are embarrassed to entertain you. Women far prefer men, unless they're one of those ineffably boring women who take it out on men for their own inadequacies; and single men of my age are so surrounded by lonely widows that you have to be thankful for the attentions of even the most unattractive of them. You go through a deep trauma and shock, yet there's no one to help you, finally, but yourself. It's gruesome!'

'Henry says there's no one to help you but God and yourself, anyway,' said Josie.

'He may be right with you as a wife,' muttered Mrs Granger, under her breath. 'Henry helps you, though. He's a marvellous husband, and you're a very lucky woman, so don't you forget it.'

June's mother retreated to the kitchen.

'What an ass Josie is!' exclaimed Mrs Granger, irritably, when her daughter had gone out of the room. 'She really does get on my nerves. She's not as bad as your mannish Aunt Bess (heaven knows how I managed to beget *her*), but she's bad enough. How about you?' She looked piercingly at June.

'Me?' asked June. 'What about me?'

'Don't you think your mother is an ass?'

'No, I don't,' replied June warmly. 'She's not the cleverest

21

in the pack, but she's a very good sort of person, and very loving too.'

'That's a dear girl!' laughed Mrs Granger. 'Now tell me what this school of yours is like. Enjoying yourself?'

To her own fury, June blushed. 'Yes,' she said. 'I simply love it.'

Mrs Granger saw the blush. 'Who's the lucky man?'

'I don't know what you mean.'

The old woman smiled. 'Are you a good actress?'

'I don't know yet.'

'You want to have a career?'

'I certainly do.'

'Good, I'm glad. I wish I'd had one, but in my day it was frowned on. Marriage was the only acceptable career – the best marriage you could make. Your grandfather was rich. He was also madly attractive. But he was hell. Never a dull moment. Affairs, affairs, affairs. And such awful women. Don't marry a man who can't be faithful, my dear. It's the most boring kind of marriage in the world.'

Josie came back with coffee. 'You two are getting on, I see! That's good, you'll be able to keep each other company.'

June was surprised. It had never occurred to her that anyone as old as her grandmother could be someone she could 'get on with'. Her grandmother was family, and simply to be tolerated – if possible. She hadn't seen much of her, as Mrs Granger had spent most of her life in Rhodesia. Disliking the threat of political change she had returned reluctantly to England, where she hated the climate and deplored the lack of help in the house. June studied her with a sudden interest and found that she liked what she saw ... a beautiful, stimulating, sharp-tongued old woman.

As things turned out, they did indeed get on, and presently came to be good friends – although June disliked her grand-mother's contempt for Josie, and found her sometimes too probing and too spoilt, and Mrs Granger found June too pliable and unassertive.

The friendship began one day when June was sitting reading in her attic bedroom. She heard a tap on the door and Mrs Granger walked in, full of apologies for 'interrupting', as she called it. She said she was bored and wanted a little chat.

June rather formally offered her a chair, and the old woman sat down, looking round her with interest.

'I like it here,' she said, as though surprised. 'It's cosy.'

'I like it, too,' said June.

'A charming rosy wallpaper, pretty furniture, and nice chintz covers on the chairs. Most attractive. What a splendid old teddy bear!'

'Yes. He's a good companion.'

Mrs Granger looked at her shrewdly. 'You know about teddy bears?'

'No? What?'

'They're a sign that you haven't grown up.'

Philip's words!

'There's plenty of time.'

'And that you don't want to grow up,' added Mrs Granger, firmly.

'This was my nursery, and I had a very happy childhood,' replied June, smiling.

'It's a lovely old house,' observed Mrs Granger. 'Pity there's no money to spend on it.'

'Yes, though it's a comfortable sort of place.'

Mrs Granger looked thoughtful. 'I'll say this for her, Josie seems to have been a good wife and mother. Even a successful one, which is more than can be said for me. I find her exasperatingly silly, but she certainly gets by in the area she has chosen for herself. It's strange, but clever men like Henry often marry stupid women. Perhaps they find it restful. Not that I should find the constant muddle in this house restful. It

23

would drive me up the wall! But there's no accounting for tastes, they say. On the other hand not everyone wants to marry a clergyman, even one as devastatingly good-looking as your father.'

'No,' said June. 'But he *is* rather beautiful, isn't he?'

'And because of his absurd calling he'll be faithful to her, lucky girl,' said Mrs Granger.

'Mother may be a muddler, but she's very comforting to have around the place,' said June warmly. 'She's been a great help to Daddy because she's so loyal, and she's so unassuming that everyone round here trusts her.'

'Trust!' murmured Mrs Granger. 'It's a magical word. And the only basis for any worthwhile relationship, don't you agree?'

Instinctively June's eye flickered towards the small photograph she had of Philip, which was on the mantelpiece. 'I don't really know,' she said.

Mrs Granger followed her glance. She got up and inspected the photograph. 'Your boyfriend?' she asked.

June flushed. 'No,' she said. 'One of the masters at school.'

'Mmm,' commented Mrs Granger. 'Quite a dish. Tall?'

'Not very.'

'I'm not altogether sure about short men,' said Mrs Granger. 'Some of them have a sense of inadequacy about their height, and it makes them think they're Napoleon.'

'He's a very good director,' said June. 'He directed one of my plays last term, and I got quite a lot of praise afterwards, and it was all his doing.' She was pleased to be talking about Philip. Just to mention his name gave her happiness, but as she hadn't said anything about him to her mother or father, she was reluctant to say too much to her grandmother.

'Your favourite tutor?'

'Yes.'

'Married?'

June hesitated. 'Yes.'

24

'Be careful, won't you, darling? Such a mistake, affairs with married men. Especially at your age. They usually end in years of wasted time if they're not just one-night stands, and I'm sure you're worth more than that.'

'Who's saying anything about affairs?' June blustered feebly.

'I am,' replied Mrs Granger. 'I'm warning you. If he's two-timing his wife he's not to be trusted, unless he's not fond of her. I should know! I had years of being the wife in among a dozen "other women". I doubt if being the other woman is a much happier state of affairs either.' She laughed without mirth. 'State of affairs is the *mot juste*,' she said. There was a silence between them, then Mrs Granger went on, 'I want you to do something for me. If you get into real trouble, like having a baby, or heading for a breakdown, let me know. I'll be here, wanting to help.'

'That's sweet of you,' exclaimed June gratefully, unwittingly giving the game away.

Mrs Granger nodded, trying to hide her smile. 'And I'd like to come and see you act, sometime. Is that possible?'

They spent a great deal of time together after this, and Mrs Granger managed to make June talk quite a lot about Philip. She, too, was able to talk freely about the dead husband she had so loved but who had proved, in her words, so negative. Both of them found release.

'Richard taught me all the more depressing facts of life,' said Mrs Granger. 'Disillusion, despair, distrust and humiliation. Don't let Philip do that to you.'

'Didn't you enjoy making love with him?' asked June.

'Certainly, but in the end it wasn't enough.'

'Then why did you stay with him?' asked June.

'At first because I adored him. Latterly because he was rich.'

'Not ever because of Mother?'

'No. To be truthful, not ever because of Josie.'

25

'Perhaps it was because of you that Mother has so little opinion of herself and makes such a muddle of everything,' said June.

'Maybe. But unhappiness sets you off balance,' replied Mrs Granger. 'That's why suicides are described as being of unsound mind.'

This shocked June into silence.

Mrs Granger left after three weeks, and Mrs Mansfield was quite clearly relieved. 'You were such a help, darling,' she said to June. 'Mother really liked you and it took such a weight off my shoulders. I wish I could get closer to her.'

'It's not your fault,' said June. 'It just happened that you and Aunt Bessie are the children of a fairly unhappy marriage.'

'I daresay, but it would be nice to be loved by one's own mother,' objected Josie.

'I'm sure she loves you,' said June, pacifically.

June's father was glad to see her go, too. 'She's not the sort of person to come home to at the end of a hard day.' He grinned. 'That mincer of a brain, and the cutting edge of her tongue, are for an idler life than mine. She's the sort of woman to break one's heart about. Not to marry.' He smiled fondly at Josie. 'Not like you, my darling,' he said.

June ruefully realised that she envied her parents their happiness.

The rest of the holiday passed pleasantly enough. June had lived in the district all her life, so she knew plenty of people. She went riding with her friends at the farm, and was asked to a couple of dances, but her mind was nearly always concerned with Philip: wondering what he was doing, and where he was. Sometimes she imagined that he loved her as much as she did him. She remembered certain phrases and some of his tenderer moments. At other times she was sure he didn't care. He had said she would be working with him again. How wonderful that would be! But would it? She had read her school report, and he had said that she had talent but must learn to concentrate, must try to have a deeper understanding of the parts she had to play. She considered and reconsidered these remarks several times a day. Was there a hidden meaning: one for her alone to decipher? She hoped so. Indeed she hoped so!

Her mother became worried about her, saying she looked pale and thin, but her father talked to her about the school so sympathetically that she longed to tell him everything. The trouble with having a clergyman for a father, she thought, was that, though most of his parishioners had no difficulty in talking to him, his own daughter wouldn't dare to tell him about an affair.

Looking back, she saw this summer as the end of her childhood.

CHAPTER FOUR

In the four terms left to her, June saw quite a lot of Philip. She did a play with him each term, and he visited her in her little room from time to time. The affair was always a frustration for her, and very often she was miserable, but the love-making itself made it all worthwhile, and she never gave up hope that one day he would learn to love her fully.

The trouble was, as she realised early on, that she was not really his type. He could only relate to a docile, dependent, and totally home-loving woman, which she recognised his wife to be. His wife was his sheet anchor. He loved her, yet he had no qualms at all about deceiving her, and he described sex as 'the jungle outside' which was 'exciting, but not a place to live in'. Anyone who knew that he was married (and he told her that he took pains before each of his affairs to explain that he was irrevocably and satisfactorily married) was having an affair with him at her own risk, he said, so the pains she might suffer were no business of his. He didn't really like talented women – in fact liking people was a rarity with him. Unusually for an actor he loathed ambition in a woman, and disapproved of the successful. But although he used them for recreation rather than for friendship, he liked being with his sort of women rather than with men, enjoying their flattery, and needing his conquest of them to boost his inadequate ego.

June saw clearly that he felt no responsibility whatever to the women he seduced, and indeed he warned her that should she ever have a baby, he would leave her at once.

He did sometimes, when he got to know her better and to trust her more, talk briefly of his family life and his upbringing. She gathered that he had disliked his mother, knowing that she had never loved him, preferring his elder brother. But this hadn't mattered as much as it might have, he said on one occasion, because when he was nine and his brother eleven, both their mother and father had been killed in an accident.

'What sort of accident?' June had asked, and he had answered evasively, 'A car accident.'

She had looked at him surprised because she thought he sounded as if he were lying. She couldn't think why he should want to lie about such a thing, but she didn't have the courage to ask.

He had then said vehemently that he had adored his father. He looked strangely haunted when he said this, but again she hadn't dared to ask him why.

After the accident he and his brother had been sent to live with an uncle and aunt who lived near Birmingham. They had had a grammar school education, and Philip had done well but had failed to get a place in a university. After a spell as an art student in Birmingham, he had drifted via an amateur group into the theatre. He said that his uncle and aunt were still alive, but that he never went to see them because he hated them. His brother still lived near them in Birmingham. When he talked of his brother he sounded bitter and jealous.

June didn't find him an admirable character, but she was kept in thrall not only by his powerful sexual attraction, but ironically by his refusal to let her become a part of his life. This, as well as his disapproval of her as a person, lacerated her pride.

Remembering these early times with him now, she wondered if, had she been less egotistical, she would have been so bound to him. Pride refused rejection, and her desire to be

29

liked by him acted as a stimulant, forging a dependence on him. But they were exciting times, too, and like everyone in love, she lived her life with a passionate intensity – each telephone call heralding heaven or hell, and a sudden sight of him affecting her like a blow to the heart. Meetings were ecstasy, absences void and desperate. Love-making was animal happiness, spiritual wonder, subservience and victory, and each day was a kaleidoscope of feeling and fantasy, of sensual gratification, of longing and fulfilment.

Luckily there was a practical bonus as well. Because she was exceedingly pretty, the male students made a play for her, and at a drama school at that time she might have had a hard time refusing to let any of them sleep with her (which with her upbringing she would have disliked doing without a strong affection) had not her liaison with Philip been well known. So she was spared the kind of one-night stands that leave a scar on the psyche, and the fumblings of experimental sex.

She had made friends with several of the other girl students and most of them, like herself, were badly off. Some were really poor (these were the days before grants) as indeed others were really rich – debutantes whose mothers treated the place as a finishing school for awkward daughters who must learn to move well and avoid bumping into the furniture.

June's set lived fairly Spartan lives. Her days were very similar, except when she was going to see Philip. She had a hurried breakfast at seven o'clock, followed by a bath, if she could get one, in one of the three bathrooms in a house of fourteen lodgers. Two bus rides took her to school (in winter, her clothes were never quite warm enough) where she worked until lunchtime, when several of the students went to a seedy café down the road if they could afford it, or had sandwiches in the cloakroom if they were broke. Lessons then resumed until the evening, with two late nights a week. Most

30

days she returned home to a supper of eggs and bacon, cooked on the gas-ring in her room, followed by a bar of chocolate. She then learned her words for the next day's rehearsal, or prepared word exercises, after which she went to bed tired, and early. Sometimes, though, she gave little suppers in her room, or went out with some of the others to their rooms, or to a pub, a club, or even the cinema. Occasionally, but most excitingly of all, they went to a play, sitting up in 'the Gods'. Not exactly a thrilling life, except to drama students, but June was happy and, when things went well with Philip, fulfilled.

She was, however, exceptionally lucky in that she saw a good deal of Granny Granger, especially at weekends when the rich old woman gave her splendid meals in her grand London flat. They were very close by this time, and Mrs Granger helped out by giving parties for June's more impecunious colleagues, and insisting on attending all their end-of-term shows. She was unaffectedly interested in their worries and joys, and never patronised them. Knowing how much she looked forward to their company, the students accepted her wholeheartedly. 'Granny Godsend' they called her, and she glowed with pleasure at the name.

She loved buying her grand-daughter clothes, and more than once took her, to her delight, to the best couturiers, also to picture galleries, concerts and the ballet. Under her guidance June's horizons broadened considerably. There was a fine library in her flat, of which June was made free. The girl lost much of her diffidence, and her grandmother's caustic humour and astringent reactions to her 'growing pains', as she called them, gave June the courage to face her reverses with some spirit. It was a profoundly satisfactory relationship for both of them.

Meanwhile at the school she was giving performances of consistently above-average quality, and in her sixth and last term she was offered a job in repertory at Worthing. She took

June Tracy as her stage name, and soon her career took off with small parts in films, and larger parts on the West End stage ...

The past receded, but June lay on in bed, thinking. All past is loss, she thought, but is all future gain? This small crisis in her life – the necessity of seeing Philip again – was like a re-introduction to the girl she had been so long ago, but from this vantage point she could hardly recognise herself. How immature she had been, and how profoundly she had loved Philip! All that was over.

But was it? Even now her imagination was polishing his image, so that her stupid heart flowered a little. The nightingale and the rose! The loving heart apparently bleeding to death on the thorn, but never in her experience quite dying; the heart's blood never quite stopping flowing; the imagination never completely at rest, nor the mind free from squirrelling its hoarded treasure.

It was absurd. Her last time with Philip, five years ago, had shown her unequivocally that they didn't match! She had found him so changed that he was without the power any longer physically to entrap her. His hands (those soft, so beautifully manicured hands) had roughened unpleasantly so that, when he took hers, she was aware of a moment of actual distaste. His face too had coarsened, and his thick brown curly hair was thinning; he was stocky, no longer lithe.

They were acting together in a play: she had the much larger part, and she could see that he didn't like this, although he behaved surprisingly well. He still seemed to like no one, except perhaps his wife. He had no friends, and a chip on his shoulder a mile wide. She had recognised all of this before, of course, but had never really acknowledged it. Now she did and, by the time the play was over, she was thankful to see the last of him. But as the years went by, his image stealthily and subtly reinstated itself in her heart, never enough to make her want to get in touch with him, but enough to make her think of him and her past love for him as the very core of her existence.

What was such a love? A quest for what? While aware of its shortcomings it yet appeared to her to be of immense importance. Why? What had she been looking for that was not totally assuaged by her feeling for Bruce – this so-much-more-worthwhile love and life with a so-much-more-worthwhile man?

When she married Bruce it had been she who was the successful one – a star. It was June for whom the telephone endlessly rang, June from whom the press wanted interviews, June in whom the world was interested. Quite soon the situation was reversed, but Bruce took his own success in his stride, never ceasing to be proud of June's. Philip, she knew, would never have been so generous. So why was she not entirely satisfied?

Bruce was more conventionally handsome. He was popular, he was kind. He loved her. He was a good companion. He was a born winner, just as Philip was fundamentally a loser. Was it this which ultimately appealed to her in a way that Bruce's more masculine self-sufficiency could not? This and Philip's consistent rejection of her as a person? Did she fundamentally need that painful and ecstatic uncertainty? And if so, why? Was it that old chestnut – a longing for something for ever out of reach? Even perhaps a pattern of longing set by her father, whose love she could never completely secure for herself since he loved her silly little mother best? Whatever it was, its insistence still dogged her.

What would this new meeting bring?

She had refused to allow Bruce to deflect her from it, and he had known, as she very well knew, that it was because of Philip she was going to stay with Mary. After all these long long years, there was yet some vital unfinished business: a

33

business so necessary for her indeed that, with her marriage to Bruce in a perhaps critical condition, she yet went ahead and accepted an invitation she knew would come between them.

Senseless. Meaningless. Irresistible.

CHAPTER FIVE

Bruce walked into the room.

'For God's sake!' he exclaimed. 'What the hell's going on?' He was still angry. 'We're to go out to lunch with the Andersons in half an hour –'

'With the Andersons? I thought there was nothing on today.'

'I told you. They called on Friday when you were at the theatre, and I accepted. You didn't say you didn't want to go.'

'I don't remember you telling me.'

'You never listen to what I have to say these days.' He was glaring at her, breathing heavily.

He had brought her to the present so forcefully that she had no reserves to meet his anger and his accusations. 'I'm sorry,' she said. 'Do you want to go on by yourself? I'll follow if you like. It won't take me long to dress.'

'I'll call them,' he said resentfully. 'Unless of course you'd rather not come?'

'No, I'd like it. Really I would.'

'What's up? Why are you still in bed? Not feeling well? Tired?' Although the words were sympathetic, he didn't sound sympathetic.

'No. I'm sorry, darling. I was miles away, and dreaming.'

'Miles away with that great bore hero of your youth?'

'I'll get dressed,' said June. 'You ring them and I'll be

35

ready in no time.' She leapt out of bed, and ran into the bathroom and he shouted after her, 'After lunch I'll drop you home, then I've got a date to discuss the play. I won't be back until late!'

June made no reply.

Bruce tidied up the Sunday papers carefully, folding them neatly and placing them with deliberate precision on the sofa table. He was still shaking with rage. He knew himself to be behaving ridiculously, but his emotions were raw, and he was unable to control them. After all these years he was still jealous of Philip, and mortally tired of his own jealousy. He knew he had nothing tangible to fear from June's visit to Suffolk, but he wanted no reminders of a situation which had come near to destroying all his happiness. He had suffered enough.

Mandy would rescue him, since June refused to do so. Mandy was kind and warm and adoring. She was far far too young for him – only two years older than his daughter – and he didn't in truth want to marry her, but she wanted him, so why not? She was clever and pretty, and quite a good actress, which would mean that she would value her independence; he couldn't bear clinging women. Perhaps a little of her youth would brush off on him, and rejuvenate him; God knows, he needed rejuvenation. For all the years of his marriage, he had worked to make June proud of him. He was now a success beyond any of his dreaming. He was rich and famous, and the critics' blue-eyed boy as well – a rare achievement. But June still eluded him. Pippa, his adored Pippa, was proud of him – but then Pippa and June had never seen eye to eye. Pippa thought her mother cold and hard and uncaring – and perhaps she was right. At all events, Bruce had had enough.

He firmly brought Mandy to mind. He was a lucky man to have her. He had met her at a party only a few months ago, and the affair had started almost at once. She was small and brunette, with an amusing triangular face. She had enormous dark brown eyes (one had a green fleck in it), short naturally curly hair, and very expressive hands which she used constantly. He and she suited each other surprisingly well. He had had several casual affairs before they met and was getting tired of them. At forty-eight he wanted to settle down emotionally, and Mandy had brought him peace. Also she had restored his self-respect, which was a gift to prize beyond all others. It was she who had pursued him, and this strangely gave him comfort. If part of the reason that she loved him was his success, so what? He had worked hard for it.

He wished he did want to marry her – it would make things so simple. But he couldn't persuade himself that it was the right thing to do; not for himself, and especially not for Mandy. He was old enough to be her father. But there was more to it than that: the truth was that, although one part of him wanted to be shot of June and the problems she created, another knew clearly that she still commanded his central loyalty; and probably always would.

He'd go to Mandy today, though, and June could stay at home alone, where she had so often left him. Pippa wouldn't be back for another fortnight. Would Pippa be pleased if he married Mandy? It was Pippa who had introduced them. She had been delighted at their affair. Had she introduced them on purpose to have some sort of revenge against June? It was possible. One day he must have a long serious talk with Pippa. One day, but not before the party. Pippa twenty-one ... How the years had flown! She was such a child still in some ways, although in others very grown up and capable. Not wise, though. Impulsive, emotional, and perhaps a little destructive. But beautiful and brilliant and loving. His only daughter!

He went to the telephone and rang the Andersons. It

37

seemed they didn't mind if he and June were late. Then he sat on the sofa at the foot of the bed, drumming his fingers on the green silk.

June came in wrapped in a towel with her soft fair hair damply clinging to her forehead. Her cheeks were pink from the heat in the bathroom, and she looked vulnerable. This touched him, which in turn made him angry again. 'Get a move on!' he said.

She dressed quickly, then put her lipstick and powder in the handbag she was taking. 'Ready!' she said, smiling. 'I'm sorry I've kept you waiting.'

He grunted some sort of non-committal reply, and she looked at him. He wasn't looking well, she thought. He was pale, and obviously upset. She ought to ring Mary and say she wouldn't come after all. But Mary was dying. Bruce should understand.

They went out into the street in silence.

The rest of the day passed in such an aura of unreality that June found it hard to make a social show of any kind. The Andersons were people whom she neither knew well, nor cared for. For some reason Bruce enjoyed their company, but to June they seemed a snobbish artificial couple. Such was their obsession with caste that all their friends and acquaintances were judged as 'par', 'above par', and 'below par'. All were classified, labelled and mentally packed in containers ready for re-examination and discussion at some later date. Each discussion entailed minute dissection of their traits and foibles, and the judgements were nearly always malicious if scurrilously entertaining. June couldn't help wondering how she and Bruce would fare after they had left, and this made her restless and self-conscious. Bruce didn't feel that way. He said their hosts' insights into people, even if not profound, were interesting, and he found them chic and amusing. He liked the food and drink they offered, and found the people

38

who came to their house stimulating and 'different from the usual theatrical mob'.

June and Bruce had walked in to find the small flat crowded and a party in full swing. The noise was deafening, and the heat excessive. Bruce was greeted as an old friend; June was complimented and flattered, but in some quite definite way given to understand that she was not a part of the group. The drinking session before lunch was prolonged and taken standing up, and the meal when it came was eaten on laps on sofas and chairs, or on the floor. It was all very uncomfortable and faux-Bohemian, but everyone looked decorative, and the food was indeed delicious.

Bruce seemed to have relaxed, which pleased her. On the way there he had been so tense and boorish that she had been quite nervous. She had never seen him boorish before. Now, surrounded and the centre of attention, he was laughing and putting himself out to charm. All she herself wanted to do was to be alone to think, but as an actress she could see that she was meant to sing for her supper. She did her best.

The party dragged on all afternoon and then, when most of the guests were leaving, it was suggested that she and Bruce should stay to drinks and supper.

'I'm afraid we can't,' she said with relief. 'Bruce told me he had another date this evening.'

'It's not important,' said Bruce at once. 'I was going to see a man about a dog, but he can wait.' And so they stayed.

They finally left at nearly midnight. June was so dead tired that she could hardly speak, and Bruce was drunk and quarrelsome.

'Another time, don't dream of putting yourself out,' he said aggressively. 'You looked so bloody bored, I was ashamed of you!'

'I tried to keep going, I really did,' said June. 'The play has been running a long time. Perhaps I'm more exhausted than I thought.'

'Yet you're willing to go to Suffolk and see Philip!'

'Mary,' corrected June. 'She's ill, I tell you.'

'Suffolk will be even more tiring than today, surely. Or won't it?'

'Oh, for God's sake! You're being childish!' June fought to keep her temper. 'Pipe down, and be your age.'

Later he tried to make love to her before they went to sleep, but she couldn't bear it, so he hurled himself out of the bedroom and spent the rest of the night in his dressing room. For the first time for many years they slept apart.

CHAPTER SIX

I have been less than honest. All that I've written here, I have written in the third person, to distance myself from the events I have described. I wanted to analyse these events as impersonally as possible; to seem the puppet master in a fictional story. But the story is no fiction. It is mine. Not 'June's'. I have lived it, suffered it, endured it, even enjoyed it. I was elated, desperate, drowned in love, unhappy beyond bearing, and happier than all future dreams are made of. But I wanted to see the people concerned in my story, myself included, through the other end of a telescope; or like actors on a stage – as removed from reality as they are at the giant O'Keefe Theatre in Toronto (where I have acted three times, and where the first few rows can see, but find it difficult to hear, and the rest of the audience can hear through mechanical aids, but find it difficult to see!). I wanted to be able to manipulate what happened, like the author of a novel, so that if reality became impossible to bear, I needn't bear it. I could be like God, or at the very least, like a Superior Being, beyond and above all that happened. Like watching an ant's nest through glass.

I am not a country woman by instinct, although I was brought up in the country. I have a kind of agoraphobia, which makes me fear the natural world while yet responding to it. I know a lot about nature, about flowers and butterflies and ants and trees, but chiefly through reading about them. Who would not be fascinated by the fact that ants yawn and stretch on waking? That in their relations with the Large Blue butterfly, ants seem venal, not to say corrupt? That trees have illnesses like flowers? That flowers feel so powerfully that they scream on being hurt? That fish have two primary emotions, lust and greed?

41

. . . There I go again. Digressing – removing my story ever further from myself, and avoiding responsibility for my past.

But I can't escape my past, any more than anyone else can. It has led inexorably to the present as it always does! I had hoped to make myself more attractive by writing about myself as some sort of heroine, but it won't do.

By the time Mary telephoned to ask me to go to Suffolk, I was so sure that I was free of my obsession with Philip that I had begun to write my story of 'June'.

Why? First and foremost, I suppose, to exorcise the ghost of Philip, but also, scarcely less important, as a confessional: to be as honest as I could about my behaviour to Bruce; to admit that much though I suffered at Pippa's hands, she had also suffered at mine. But the aim and value of this confession was debased for the reader and for myself if I was saying in effect 'It wasn't me . . . it was June.' It was me . . . let that be quite clear from now on.

I think if I were asked to describe the difference between loving and being in love, I would say the 'imagination factor'. The person with whom we are in love is the one who corresponds most nearly to our most profound desires and fantasies, which are the fruits, I really believe, of early influences, early maladjustments. Falling in love may be an instinctive attempt to correct such maladjustments, and so depends on an inner imagination. Is this why the course of true love hardly ever runs smooth; why it can end in tragedy, and why it can affect us more deeply and dangerously than a less complicated love can do?

I was in love with Philip in this way – but Philip's love for me was only sexual. I doubt if even at the best of times, and times were lovely now and then, he truly loved me on any other plane at all. He was also married to the dullest little woman imaginable. That is, she seemed dull to me. She was clever and humourless, and had made herself Philip's loyal shadow. Without him she could not have existed, and, though I hate to admit it, without her Philip might have ceased to exist in any form acceptable to himself. I suppose therefore she must have conformed to *his* most urgent needs, as he once did to mine. I loved Bruce, then as now, as a friend, as a companion, as the saviour of my reason when I had reached my nadir, and as a husband and the father of my child. I had no right then to go on this trip to Suffolk, which would alienate him still further, even though a dying Mary had asked me to see her. Bruce was dead against it, and so would Pippa be, when she returned. And it would strengthen still further her steel-strong bonds with her father.

Pippa . . . there was a riddle for me! A conundrum which I had never set myself to solve because it had always seemed too difficult! And yet unless I solved it, I should do her less than justice; and might already have maimed her capacity for loving by my reluctance to take the matter firmly in hand. It couldn't be good for her to have this one-sided view of family life. She had made us into a one-parent family – with a father only. She and Bruce were family. I was the unwanted stranger in their midst . . . not even the hired help . . . and the fact that I brought her into the world made her if anything dislike me more. (This began very early, so early, indeed, that her first word being Dada, she declined for years to add Mama to her vocabulary!)

She was a beautiful baby, a beautiful little girl, and she is now a beautiful young woman. From the first she preferred men, and her favourite man was inevitably her father. It was my own fault that he encouraged her. Bruce had met me just when Philip had abandoned me. As my feelings for Philip were by no means over, it was only natural that at first Bruce felt frustrated in our relationship. He thought he came second best, not realising that as a friend and husband he was first and always first. When Pippa was born we both thought our troubles would be over. Bruce adored Pippa. He was glad that she was a girl, astounded at her beauty, ravished by her obvious intelligence. He was the proud father taken to the nth degree. With him she never cried, never threw tantrums, always set out to charm.

It was extraordinary how early she realised how to charm him! Her smile for him was always warmer, sweeter, than her smile for anyone else. From the moment she could walk she followed him around the house doggedly and with the utmost good humour if not deflected from her purpose. When he sat in his study, writing, she would sit there watching him for hours, utterly silent and so withdrawn that she didn't upset his concentration. She listened absorbed as in a kind of trance when he talked, and obeyed immediately when he gave commands. Bruce found all this enchanting.

I found it slightly less so. It seemed unnatural to me then, and it still seems so now. She seldom played childish games, unless to show her dolls and toys to her father. She loved to hear him telling stories, and later she would make up stories for him that pleased and flattered him – but she never included me. She was brought to the theatre where I was playing once or twice, but seemed to hate it: she was restless when I was on the stage, and bored when I wasn't, so she soon ceased to come. It is almost impossible to describe the pain this indifference and exclusion caused me.

I had not expected to feel maternal (nor had Bruce expected it) but I enjoyed the prospects of motherhood inordinately and indeed, in spite of her neglect of me, for the first few years of her life I was as besotted about Pippa as was Bruce. I was not domesticated in other ways, but then I did not have to be. We had enough money to pay for help in the house, and I was always lucky. My helpers became my friends, advisers, and except about Philip, my confidantes. They stayed for years, and in a very real sense became part of the family, all the more so since they had been chosen with care when they were engaged, and so had an advantage over awkward relations.

44

Both my parents were still alive at this time, and they too idolised my clever daughter. She, of course, preferred her handsome grandfather, but she behaved with great decorum towards my mother, who had no idea how she was being manipulated. She was always bringing Pippa little presents – never expensive, because she couldn't afford them, but gifts which always seemed to be exactly what the child wanted.

Although he loved her dearly, my father was not uncritical of her. Like Bruce he was a wonderful storyteller; he had endless patience with her, and he enjoyed reading aloud the kind of books she loved. I can see him yet, in his high-backed armchair by the fireside, his clear-cut profile etched palely against the dark panelling, his thick silky white hair made slightly rosy by the light diffused by a red lamp-shade, his still-dark eyebrows lifted in amusement at the tale he was communicating. His voice was soft, mandarin, and with the slightly sing-song cadences of his calling. Pippa sitting on a cushion on the floor beside him listened as she always did, in an almost exaggeratedly focused way. They made a group fit only for great painting to immortalise – a picture so perfect that in lesser hands it might seem sentimentally posed. Was Pippa self-conscious even so young? Did she even then know the effects of her appearance? Hard to tell. I hope not.

I have made her sound obnoxious perhaps – a prodigy, a caricature – but of course she was none of these things. Doubtless she thought of me in equally exaggerated terms. The fact is, I found her incomprehensible – yet I felt responsible for the way she was, so my love was distorted by anxiety.

I know only too well that I forfeited her love for me when I reopened my affair with Philip. What I can't understand is how she could judge me so harshly at such a tender age, and how she could sustain such a coldness towards me for so long. We are mother and daughter, not strangers, and I know I couldn't judge her so brutally, whatever she did. Her animosity has made me see her faults more clearly, but it can never extinguish my love.

Granny Godsend loved her too – and heaven knows, she was a shrewd enough observer. If she had lived, perhaps she could have guided me with Pippa, as she guided me in so much else. As it was, Pippa grew up entirely in the way that she thought would most please Bruce. From an early age she was passionately keen on clothes and had an instinctive flair for wearing them. Her taste ran to demure, very feminine frilly dresses, and Bruce loved to see her wearing such things. (He sometimes treated her like a little doll, and she thoroughly enjoyed it.)

Besides her feminine clothes, her close concentration on his every move, and the mannerisms she cultivated to enchant him, Pippa decided to be the tidiest, best behaved, best mannered little girl in the world – at home. At school she was different: excelling at lessons but, out of class, wilful and disobedient. 'A bewildering pupil,' her headmistress reported. 'I cannot predict a stable future for her.' But she enjoyed school. Perhaps she was more nearly her true self there, and found relief from the non-stop performance she put on for Bruce ...

Her precocious social ease was a great success with our friends. They always found her charmingly 'natural', and 'no trouble at all'. But she wasn't charmingly natural. The whole of her persona was studied and artificial. Daddy's little girl was made up out of her head in the most calculating manner imaginable, and about everyone else but Daddy she was as cold as ice. She had no friends of her own age, but she fooled Bruce completely, together with all our own friends.

You see? I didn't understand her, and I disapproved. That can't have been any easier for her than it was for me.

It was a strange and most unchildish childhood I now realise, but it seemed to satisfy Pippa; and by the time she had grown up she had almost complete control over her dual personality, and a self-discipline astonishing in one so young. The snag was that she had no idea what to do with herself after school. Bruce was the be-all and end-all of her bizarre life, and having won all the prizes except the position of Head Girl, she seemed to want to live at home for ever, basking in his praise and love. At last even Bruce tried to take a stand.

'But you must do something, my darling! We won't always be here, you know, to look after you, and we want to be sure that you'll be able to look after yourself when we're gone. Besides, you are so clever! You can't let it all go to waste. You must choose what you want to do, and we'll move heaven and earth to see that you get it.'

But all Pippa did was burst into tears and beg him not to talk about dying . . .

During the five weeks following Pippa's return, the preparations for her party went forward ceaselessly. She seemed very excited about it. She had bought herself a lovely new black velvet dress in which she looked a dream, and the choice of the food and the flowers was entirely hers.

She and I had made up the guest list together, but she filed all the acceptances herself. She managed to keep me at arm's length, although we had to work closely together. And I was right. She was very angry that I was going to visit Philip and Mary. Sometimes I had the uneasy feeling that she had a new and more determined ambition to come between Bruce and me; that she wanted to oust me not only from his affections, but ultimately from his life. Was this why she had introduced Bruce to Mandy? And why she relished their affair? I doubted if she wanted to see them married, because that would mean the break-up of her home and an end to her main aim in life – to keep Bruce for herself. Mandy was only to divide us in our affection, not in our home.

Or so I thought.

CHAPTER SEVEN

One morning in 1957, I had a telephone call from my agent to say that I had been offered two jobs simultaneously, both in the theatre. One was a good, intellectual piece in London, to be directed by a reputable director, for Binkie Beaumont of H. M. Tennent (at that time the most important management in London); the other was to star opposite Philip, in *Tea and Sympathy*, in South Africa. Obviously I should have chosen the London play. Really good new plays with something to say are thin on the ground, as are good directors, and Binkie didn't offer me jobs all that often. But I was still in love with Philip, and to my agent's horror, settled for South Africa.

Professionally it was a foolish thing to do, and might well have done me incalculable harm in the future had Binkie been the kind of man to hold grudges. Which he wasn't. All the same it was a great opportunity missed, and my agent took a long time to forgive me. I didn't mind, however. Try as I might, I couldn't rid myself of my obsession for Philip, and the chance of spending three months, day in and day out, in his company was too exhilarating to turn down. I had no idea if Mary would be coming out too, but I was so besotted that I would have preferred even that to forgoing the opportunity to be with him.

Philip was kinder to me by that time, although he didn't see me often since they lived out in Hertfordshire. His excuse was that he couldn't get away from her. I knew that he wasn't

48

any more faithful to me than he was to Mary, but I was still hooked. He created a magic which no other man ever created for me. Being in bed with him represented the greatest happiness I have ever experienced. To me he was a soul mate – a predestined partner – and I couldn't understand why he thought of me as alien.

I pondered the problem over and over again. How could I be foreign to him, when I was so pliable, so uncritically loving, and so harmless? Now, of course, I see why. To him I represented danger: I attracted him too strongly for comfort, and he didn't want me to break up his marriage.

Charlie Stewart, another boyfriend, came down to Heathrow to see me off. I was expecting to see Mary with Philip, and the thought of witnessing their marital farewell had worried me, but there was no sign of her. Philip seemed preoccupied when I introduced Charlie; however, once airborne his mood soon changed. We had been put together in first class, and all the rest of the company in economy, and this clearly delighted Philip in spite of his socialist principles. We had champagne together, and several people recognised us; all of which he enjoyed. I thought him beautiful, and I was not the only one. The stewardesses did too, and he flirted with them outrageously. Seeing him so relaxed gave me absurd happiness.

But rehearsals in Johannesburg produced another change of mood. My part in *Tea and Sympathy* was much better than his – not easy for my former teacher – and what's more he had to play a homosexual, which he disliked. He had accepted the job out of necessity, and knew that I had not, and this angered him; and as usual when he was angry he took it out on me; and the way he always took it out on me was to make a play for someone else near me. It never failed to make me unhappy, and this gave him satisfaction: he had power over me, and could demonstrate it. There was only one other woman in the cast (the stage management was all male, so

49

that they could also understudy as there were so many men in the play), and she was exceedingly, almost comically unattractive – but that didn't worry him. He liked plain women (some obscure sort of revenge against pretty ones, I suppose).

For some years British Equity had been insisting that all shows involving its members going out to South Africa had to be available to blacks as well as whites. By now it was on the point of decreeing that blacks and whites must be allowed to attend the same performances. I had expected Philip to insist on this here and now, and when he didn't, I asked the management myself. To my surprise, Philip didn't back me up. I now see that he didn't want to risk jeopardising the engagement. To my delight, the management agreed and arranged for half a dozen shows in various halls throughout the country where blacks and whites could come together; and so a magical thirteen weeks' work was mapped out for us.

I don't quite know when Philip decided to soften his attitude towards me, or indeed why. Perhaps the other girl, who was a tiresome aggressive creature, proved too much for him? Or perhaps the fact that I had chosen him, not Binkie, had had a good effect although initially making him angry. Anyway, quite soon he seemed suddenly to be fond of me again, and of course I was entranced – literally. Indeed, I often felt that I was under a spell with Philip. For instance I invariably guessed, when the telephone rang, if the caller was Philip. I was almost always free if he wanted to see me (sometimes under the oddest circumstances, when I had previously been booked but the date was changed at the last moment). If I telephoned Philip at home (which he hated), I never got Mary, always Philip. Over and over again I had the most vivid feeling of *déjà vu* – that what I now experienced was a kind of re-run of something that had already happened. Never instinctively religious, in spite of my family background, I became convinced that the whole thing was pre-

50

ordained – a new, unique and enduring conviction in my experience.

So now, to know that we had thirteen uninterrupted weeks ahead of us was like paradise. I prayed that the tour would be a joyous one, and my prayers were answered. We had weeks and weeks of unalloyed pleasure, and during those weeks Philip was the ideal companion. It was the peak of my happiness in life. Nothing else has ever come anywhere near it (although that is not to say that I haven't found happiness since).

Why was I so happy?

To begin with, South Africa is probably the most beautiful country I have seen. I had been expecting an arid brown landscape, under sunny bright blue skies. Instead much of it is green and lush, and in the eternal sunshine (extra prized because in England it would be midwinter), without any sense of responsibility towards the friends and family we had left behind, Philip and I became close at last – though not close enough, as I found out later.

If the days were magical, the nights were even more wonderful. The skies glowed with outsize stars, so crisply brilliant against the soft indigo canopy curving over the darkened world that they seemed almost within reach; and with all restraints removed, Philip and I made love, oh such love, night after night after night.

In Johannesburg we were immediately engulfed in the lavish but exhausting 'good life' of endless hospitality. We ate, drank and were merry, and found it hard to think of the victims of apartheid. Occasionally, though, sitting quietly with our generous hosts after a marathon drinking session, we or they would raise the subject, and we would be given the standard defence of Government policy. 'The blacks are children, not yet ready for political responsibility. Look what is happening in the rest of Africa! If things are so bad for them here, why should thousands be trying to get in to South

51

Africa from outside? They earn better money here, that's why. We build houses for them far better than anything they would build for themselves. But they prefer their rotting shanty towns, and riot when we make them leave them. The world press is always saying that we took their land away from them, but in fact the Xhosa tribe – who now make up the bulk of the black population – are no more indigenous than the whites. They too fought the aboriginal bushmen to win their place in the sun, and at roughly the same time as the whites. They then fought the white settlers and lost, but it was never their land so why should they get preferential treatment? Besides, with their nomadic way of life they graze the land until it becomes desert, and then move on to create more desert.'

However sincerely and even plausibly expressed, and however often we heard it, this was an argument impossible to accept, and to me the crowning irony of the South African tragedy is that the strongest protagonists of apartheid and all its attendant evils claim to be devout Christians. But I must confess that all this was no more than a sombre background to the story of my love for Philip.

From Johannesburg we went to Cape Town through the Big and Little Karoos. The company manager had hired a car for us, which Philip drove. We took three idyllic days on our thousand-mile journey, making it a little holiday. Time out. One day we had a puncture in the wide spaces of the Little Karoo, and Philip reluctantly got out of the car to change the wheel. A huge young Boer farmer who was passing in his truck saw us and kindly told us to come down to his farm where he would send one of his 'boys' out to see to our car, and would give us lunch. Gratefully we accepted his lift. We went down a long badly kept road to the enormous sprawling ugly house, and it was an extraordinary interlude – a nightmare vision of male chauvinism.

The farmer's wife told me that I mustn't eat in the dining

room, but with her in the kitchen. Like the whole family she spoke English with a hideous guttural Afrikaner accent. In the drawing room where I was only allowed to stay for a few minutes, there were rows and rows of silver-framed photographs on all the flat surfaces, all of them of relations both living and dead. The room was drab and crowded with enormous stuffed sofas and chairs; so overstuffed indeed that they looked obscene. The rest of the furniture was made of a wood like oak; a few upright chairs with wooden seats, two side tables with lamps on, a gatelegged sofa table, and that was all. There were no flowers, but more faded sepia photographs on the walls; not of people, but landscape.

The farmer and two others were present, giants of men. All had red faces, and the farmer's nose was veined from too much drink. It was a moist nose, and his over-large big-lipped mouth was wet and red. The other men were like him, but quite handsome – fair-haired and lean. The farmer offered Philip a drink then nodded to his wife to take me away.

When we reached the kitchen the woman said in a resigned and whining voice, 'You see? That's how it is! We're millionaires and that's my life! Stuck here with that lot! They talk about the farm all the time, or about the "kaffirs" – our dear servants who serve us so faithfully – and they seduce their women while despising them and hating themselves afterwards for being "unclean". They think they might get diseases from sleeping with them, but they never think of the wretched women having to bring up the bastards they father on them! It's disgusting and I hate it all! I'd like to kill the lot of them, but like the blacks here I'm only a servant. I work for them, and minister to them, and now because I'm old and have lost my looks, I'm no longer close to any of them. They haven't a shred of affection for me. I hate them with such passion that it gives me the only pleasure I know. Imagine! I'm a millionairess and I wait on them at table and have no clothes, no fun, and spend my life here in the kitchen! And all of them believe in God and the Bible, and call themselves puritans. I could vomit!'

She was angular and mean-looking with dry frizzed hair, nearly grey now, but showing traces of having been fair. Her cheeks were browny red like rotting harvest apples, and her small eyes were a piercing blue.

The lunch she served them could have fed a dozen men: huge helpings of soup, red meat, dumplings, vegetables and baked and roast and mashed potatoes – all washed down with beer, and followed by enormous treacle puddings, then platefuls of bread and cheese. So much in that ugly house was on a gargantuan scale.

It was a strange couple of hours, and I was glad when we were once more on our way; but Philip had enjoyed himself. I couldn't understand it. I can only suppose that he found this evidence of accepted male domination reassuring even in such an extreme form. I didn't know then what an effort he continually had to make to reconcile the chaos of his past with the apparent order of his present. Mary was his life-line – the janitor of his sanity. I was never even offered a skeleton key.

In Cape Town, Philip and I alone of the company stayed at the splendid old Mount Nelson Hotel, a large white colonial structure with pillars. The rooms were large and airy, the gardens beautifully kept, and the food good. The other residents were all old at this time, and seemed to resent the fact that we were young. We didn't care. The play had been a success in Johannesburg, but here it didn't go down too well. Cape Town was less sophisticated than Johannesburg and a play about homosexuals was not to their taste at all, although they thought they ought to like what they thought of as a 'highbrow' play, so the houses were packed.

Philip didn't like the Mount Nelson, because he couldn't bear the thought of the Empire; and he didn't like Cape Town, because he said it smacked of colonialism, Dutch as well as English; but he did seem to love me at this time, and like any actor, he enjoyed having full houses. He also enjoyed our visits to new friends on a wine farm at Groot Drakenstein – friends who had a passion for the theatre, a lovely Dutch house with good pictures, acquaintances able to hold interesting conversations, and a first-class swimming pool.

From Cape Town we took the lovely Garden Route to Port Elizabeth and East London in the Eastern Province of the Cape. Then, on our way north to Durban, we played one-night stands in the little townships of King William's Town and Queenstown. These are set in a broad landscape of rolling hills with a backdrop of mountains, the closest dark blue in that crystalline air, and behind them range upon range of ever paler blue, until the most distant merge into the sky.

In Zululand, which is more tropical, there are waterfalls on the Insusi River, behind which you can sit on little ledges in the welcome shade of a smooth green curtain of water. Huge lilies and red-hot pokers stalk down the green hillsides; shocking pink, violent yellow and blazing white pig-flowers bloom everywhere and the rich mournful singing of the Zulu women – the men are away in the Johannesburg mines – can be heard from the clusters of their whitewashed thatched rondavels under the scarlet-flowered trees.

Oh, South Africa – what a 'beloved country' indeed! How often, when sickened by your tensions and grieving and violence, have I yet thought with gratitude of my time there with Philip.

Obsession is extraordinary. It absorbs the mind and spirit so utterly that one can only hope to be released from it by reliving the circumstances that inspired it, and with luck discovering them to be irrelevant to the living present. Without my knowing it, Philip was suffering from an obsession as

55

urgent as mine; and a far more profound and frightening one. I might have been able to help him had I known. Certainly I would have understood our relationship more clearly. In the circumstances it was a miracle that he relaxed with me as much as he did. Perhaps – who knows? – I was a small life-line after all. Not as valuable as Mary, but having my uses. He needed vulnerable women – he had an instinct for them – and with hindsight I realise how valuable that instinct was for him then. I only knew that, during that marvellous time, I didn't pose any threat. He didn't have to conquer me in making love, and he didn't try to reject me.

I had noticed that he often spoke in clichés, and sometimes I acknowledged secretly that, had I not been so in love with him, I would have found him a slight bore. I realise now that clichés reassured him. They were timeworn and self-evident truths which posed him no problems; didn't need to be tested to be trusted. Because, of course, in general a lack of trust dogged him and damned him. And no wonder! In South Africa he was free of it. Although many beautiful girls wanted him, as they had always wanted him throughout the time I had known him, he had no need to demonstrate his masculinity or his self-control by sleeping with them. Only with me. Only with me.

Love! Flesh worshipping flesh. The mind and spirit alive and joyous in the simultaneous experience of wild excitement and total peace. Every nerve-end tingling with feeling, the emotions in permanent fluctuation. Desire melting into satiation, which turns again to desire and satiation. All dreams fulfilled. What a time it was! Perfection – perfection – body and spirit fused, and the world filled with glory.

Exhaustion, too. I've never been so drugged with tiredness! Some evenings I could hardly force myself through the long part I had to play on the stage; but the sight of Philip, so handsome in his make-up (and ironically playing my husband), pulled me through – although as a trained

56

actress I should have given a decent performance anyway, I hope.

The memory of that tour is a memory of bodies. Philip's – beautiful, compact, with wide shoulders, slim hips and dark hair on his chest; mine – glowing and obedient to him and performing its proper function for me as a woman. All woman at last! In bed – in the warm sea – in streams and pools made by waterfalls in the countryside – under trees and on the hillsides. Bodies. His and mine.

Philip never seemed to tire of me, nor I of him. He never scolded me, and we even talked sometimes after our loving, although we never mentioned his problem, his marriage – and almost never, Mary. For me it was enough to have been granted a sight of heaven. I lived each day entirely for the present.

The end when it came was absolutely unexpected, sending me into a pit of despair so deep that I nearly lost my reason. Suicide beckoned, but it only beckoned: I'm a survivor by instinct, and luckily my instinct was strong.

Our final week of special performances before mixed audiences entailed a tiring programme of visiting a new township every day. Philip and I travelled together by car, while the rest of the company went with the company manager by bus, and the scenery travelled in a large pantechnicon driven by a Cape-coloured. By six o'clock the scenery was in position. At half-past we walked round the set to familiarise ourselves with any changes necessitated by the size of the new hall, and tested out the acoustics, sometimes even rehearsing a scene from the play. At seven we were making up, and at seven-thirty we started. And to my satisfaction a few blacks could be seen in the audiences.

But now the whole company stayed in the same lodgings; a small hotel perhaps, or with friends of the management, who had large houses; anywhere that could be found – and Philip

57

became reluctant to continue our affair. 'Not fair on Mary,' he said. 'I don't want the company talking.'

'But they must have been talking all the time!' I objected.

'Only surmise. They can't prove anything.'

'Why should they want to?' But it was no use.

'Not fair to Mary,' he said. And that was that.

On the last night before leaving for England, I knocked on the door of his room.

A wary voice called, 'Come in'.

I went in, wearing my nightdress and dressing gown.

Philip, fully clothed, was sitting at a table, writing. He looked at me coldly. 'Yes?' he asked.

'It's our last night,' I said.

'I know.'

'So I wondered if we could spend it together,' I said.

'I told you. No. I don't want Mary hurt.'

'But we may not see each other for some time.'

'So?'

'Hasn't it been as wonderful for you as it has for me?' I asked.

'I've enjoyed it, certainly.'

'Enjoyed it?' I echoed, stunned. 'Is that all it has meant to you?'

'What else should it have meant?' he asked.

'Surely you love me, as I love you?'

'I told you, love is a disease, like lust.'

I didn't understand, and said in bewilderment, 'But this time together has been perfection!'

'I'm glad,' he said. 'Something to look back on.'

'Hasn't it been perfection for you?'

'Perfection is a pretty big word,' he said. 'I've told you I've enjoyed it.'

'Nothing more?' I could feel the tears coming to my eyes, and a constriction in my throat.

'Look,' said Philip. 'I'm a married man. You've been after

58

me ever since we met. Mary is my wife. You know that. I've never made any secret of the fact that I am married, and that I shall never leave my wife. If you fall for a married man you get what you deserve. If you've liked what you've got, you should consider yourself a lucky girl.' He'd said something of the sort before, but after such weeks of loving I could hardly believe my ears.

'Won't you want to see me when we get back to England?' I demanded.

'Well I shan't want to make dates, if that's what you mean! Of course if Mary goes away, and we still fancy each other, perhaps we can meet, but we can't bank on it.'

I gazed at him helplessly. Finally I said, 'Will you sleep with other women sometimes?'

He looked back at me apparently amazed. 'Well of course I will,' he said. 'Why ever not? I always have.'

I was appalled. 'Won't Mary mind?' I asked.

He grinned, and suddenly looked cruel. 'We don't exactly have chats on the subject,' he replied, and laughed, shortly. 'Now you must hop it,' he added. 'Someone may hear us.'

'Would you kiss me once, Philip? Please? Just once?'

'Not now,' he said.

'Will you ring me sometimes when we get back home?' I asked, desperate now.

'I may. I've no idea.'

'I may ring you, now, after this, mayn't I?' I said.

'After what? And no, you certainly may not! No phone calls. No letters. No nothing. We've had a good time. The good time has come to an end. If we ever work together again, and we still want to, perhaps we'll take up where we left off. Why not? I've enjoyed it, I tell you. Otherwise, nothing. Mary is owed some peace of mind. She's a good girl.'

'But Philip ...' I protested.

He suddenly became impatient – 'Oh for God's sake!' he exclaimed. 'Look outward, angel! The world isn't just made

59

up of you and me. There's poverty, starvation, murder, rape, mutilation, baby battering, drugs and homelessness – to name but a few things. You're a clergyman's daughter – yet the outside world never touches you. Love is OK in its place, but it's not the alpha and the omega of living. Buzz off darling. It's late and I'm very very tired.'

I left the room in tears.

So we went back to England, and I didn't see him again for many years.

CHAPTER EIGHT

I have said little up to this point about Mary; but then to me she was always the interloper, although of course in their eyes it was I who was that. I could never totally believe that Philip could prefer her, and on the first occasion I met her (backstage, after one of Philip's productions at dramatic school) I couldn't imagine what he had ever seen in her. She had already lost her looks, and seemed worn and tired. Emaciated, with a rubbery skin, she was in her early thirties when we met but seemed far more. She had grey streaks in her dark curly hair, and a small, rather pointed nose. Her brown eyes were small, and her unmade-up lips were meagre, though sensitively shaped. She and Philip had met in repertory, but when they married she had given up the stage. It was rumoured that she had a little private money, some pretensions to an academic background, a sister whom she loathed, and parents whom Philip couldn't stand. She was humourless, but an excellent housekeeper, and her whole life was wrapped up in Philip. Once years later I met someone who had known her in her repertory days. She had been pretty, he said, and very vivacious; always laughing. She seldom laughed on the rare occasions I met her.

This makes it sound as if her life with Philip had already subdued her. It may have, but I don't think it was entirely Philip's fault. It was her own wish to live entirely through him; to be his slave, his keeper, his shadow and his efficient housekeeper. Somehow she had found a way to keep her

61

extremely difficult husband bound to her for life. How she had managed to get him to trust her after what he had been through, I don't know. Timing, perhaps. The girl he loved before he met Mary had laughed at his troubles – Mary had rescued him, and he was generous enough not to resent being grateful.

Mary was invariably nice to me, and I have to acknowledge that her manners were considerably better than my own – but then she had all I wanted . . . marriage to Philip. It was all she wanted, too.

When Philip left me after South Africa I was a lost soul. Some people believe that the only hell we shall know is hell on earth: I hope so. I certainly knew what hell was then, the more so because, after all, and despite all his caution, someone told Mary of our affair. Philip telephoned me to say so, and asked me if it had been me. Naturally, I denied it, furiously.

'Then who?' he asked.

'How the hell should I know? And how the hell could you think such a thing of me?'

'Well, *someone* has let the cat out of the bag,' he said flatly. 'Bastards! Mary was extremely upset. I've denied it of course, and after a massive row or two I think I've managed to convince her, but it has been touch and go. Well I'm glad it wasn't you. It wouldn't have been a very nice thing to do.'

'I thought you trusted me!' I said, almost crying.

'No one can be completely trusted when they are in love,' he answered. 'They're always slightly crazy.'

This shocked me even more, but I said, 'I promise you I wouldn't dream of letting you down, sane or crazy! You must believe me! Please!'

He gave a strange little grunt, then said, 'Well this puts paid to seeing one another again, doesn't it? Not that we've got much chance, as it turns out.'

62

'Why? If we're careful no one would know.' I was desperate. 'Why does this make it impossible to meet?'

'It's not worth the risk,' he answered.

'I see,' I replied, sick at heart. 'Not worth the risk.'

'No. So take care of yourself, and thanks for the memory, lover girl.'

Not surprisingly I felt even worse after this, if that were possible. Now I was really on my own. I suddenly realised that because of Philip, no matter how seldom I had seen him, I had never been irrevocably alone. I had gone to dramatic school straight from home, and had met him in my second term. On and off we had been seeing each other ever since. He had filled my life even if he wasn't with me; and now, and with no hope, I was abandoned. I had to drag myself out to do my shopping, and housework was an effort almost too great to be made. Sleep was a nightmare chase, the simplest chores took me three times longer than they should – and of course I was also out of work. I had chosen Philip and South Africa: the girl playing 'my' part in the hugely successful Tennent production had been offered a film contract by MGM, but nobody seemed to want me.

I was determined not to give in totally to my despair, however, and in my misery turned to my grandmother. She was a tower of strength; how lucky I was! She was strong and true and understanding, always loving, and always there when I needed her. Once, though, I turned up at her house having had too much to drink, and she was furious with me.

'You ought to be ashamed of yourself!' she said. 'It's a coward's way out, to drink. I can't stand self-pity! Courage is what life is all about. Anyway, you know what I think about this little man of yours. He's hell. Worse than Richard, who at least married me and supported me. He's no good to you, as I've told you a thousand times before, and you're very well off without him. Absurd to waste yourself on him. You're beautiful and talented, and once he's out of your system you'll find some nice boy and settle down. I know you will.'

'You never found a substitute for Richard.'

'I was his wife.'

'I don't think one ever finds a substitute for one's real love,' I said.

She answered slowly, 'You may be right, but you have to try. Romantic love is a hangover from an earlier stage of evolution, and totally useless now, like an appendix.'

'Do you ever wish that Richard was still alive?' I asked.

'How do I know? Yes – no, I'm sure I don't. I don't know. Perhaps.'

She was twisting the huge rings on her long fingers impatiently. My heart ached for her. He'd died so long ago, and she was still in such distress.

She gave dinner parties for me and now she invited all the young men she could get hold of to meet me, the grandsons of friends or friends of friends. She took infinite care to see that I shouldn't feel totally bereft. She telephoned me several times a week to find out how I was getting on, and called on me from time to time if she 'happened to be passing', even when it was transparently clear that I was well off her way. She cherished me and spoiled me, and kept a loving watch over me, and through her I won through. Then one day, months later, I met Bruce.

I remember the day quite clearly, and I remember the conviction I had from the moment I saw him that he was somehow important to me. It wasn't at one of my grandmother's parties after all, but at, of all things, a friend's cocktail party. I hate them, and I'd only accepted because I was going on to dinner in a house nearby. An actress friend of mine was determined to get to know a certain television director whose girlfriend she knew, so had invited them to drinks.

Bruce came alone. He was only an acquaintance, a struggling young writer who lived in the same block of flats,

64

and she forgot to introduce us. But I noticed him at once: he was easily the most attractive man in the room. And from the moment he saw me, he made a play for me. He told me I was beautiful, that he admired my work, and that he'd fallen in love with me when he'd seen me playing Olivia in *Twelfth Night*. I'd heard the same sort of thing from other men, but he said his piece with such controlled ferocity that, although I found it a little unnerving, I believed him and was flattered.

He pursued me ardently during the next few weeks with flowers, telephone calls and chocolates. I thought this delightfully old-fashioned, but he was good company when we met. We had dinner together several times, and I was impressed by his charming manners and his choice of modest but excellent eating places. Nearly everything that I heard about Bruce was in his favour, although everyone said he was difficult to know well. He was easy to talk to, and I suddenly found that I was actually thinking of him more than I was brooding on Philip. He had interested me enough to make enquiries about him, and from finding his pursuit of me slightly ludicrous, I began to look forward to the telephone calls and flowers, and to miss them when they didn't come. This brought me up with a jerk. Was I falling in love with him? I really believed that I was.

It was inevitable that he would ask me to marry him, but I wasn't too keen to take anybody on the rebound, so told him about Philip. He was very sympathetic, but didn't stop pursuing me, and finally I gave in.

I took him to see my grandmother and was enormously relieved when she told me she liked him. 'Just the sort of man I would have chosen for you myself,' she said. 'Take care of him. He's one in a million, child.' I wondered a little that she told me to take care of him.

She and Mother and Father came to the wedding, and Mother and Father approved too. Fortunately Bruce seemed equally enthusiastic about them, and Granny took to nannying him, as she had nannied me. Until she died a few years later, she was constantly in our lives.

After the wedding we moved into my flat, because his was small and gloomy. This was one of my mistakes: it must have made him feel inadequate that he couldn't provide for me the things I wanted. Another mistake was the way I told him about Philip. I made him out to have been the love of my life – how could I help it? – and this must have been hard to swallow. The truth was that the timing wasn't right. Bruce had come into my life too soon after my rejection, and Philip was still in the forefront of my mind. Again when, quite soon, I found myself loving Bruce for himself, and not for the fact that he had saved me from despair, I should have made it plainer; but I thought he must know it, as he was usually so sensitive to other people's emotions. So many mistakes, and in the end I paid! But not until I had made the greatest mistake of all.

For eight years we were happy. We were good companions, our loving was good, and we had Pippa. Everything seemed to unite to give us fulfilment in a stable marriage. Perhaps I had it too easy. My career went steadily upwards; if not spectacularly, at least with work of which I had no need to be ashamed. So did Bruce's. We were comfortably off, we both adored our child, and we travelled a lot. We should have been able to keep the marriage going, but we failed. It was my fault. My stupid fault. Those eight years were good years, the most worthwhile I've had so far. I was very fortunate, but too spoilt to know my own luck.

CHAPTER NINE

The year 1980 was a watershed for me. The run-up to Pippa's twenty-first birthday was hectic and complicated and very soon things turned sour. Neither Pippa nor I knew it then, but Bruce was having a difficult time with Mandy. He had agreed to divorce me, but refused to tell me so before Pippa's birthday, because he thought I already had enough on my plate. Mandy had no need to feel insecure once Bruce had made up his mind to leave me, but she clearly wanted to grab him while the going was good, and refused to accept his reason for the delay.

As far as I could see, her hang-up was that she had come from a small suburban background and was ashamed of it. Bruce was not only a sexy and handsome man, he had wealth and fame, and above all a social ease which she admired. He was also an intellectual and this satisfied a craving in her for the type of education she had missed. That he was older was no deterrent, any more than it had been for me with Philip; in fact in her case it was a considerable advantage. Beyond her ambitions as an actress was a desperate fear of failure, and Bruce represented security. She had set her cap at him, and to her amazement he had responded. She willed herself to be in love with him, because he was so exactly the sort of man she was looking for; and by the time of the party, she imagined that she was. His delay in making the announcement genuinely scared her: she had so little faith in her attractions that she thought it meant she was losing him, and she couldn't bear it. She made constant scenes and nearly lost him. As she never really explained her anxieties, but only endlessly repeated her wish for an announcement of the engagement at this particular time, Bruce found the whole thing incomprehensible and distasteful. Their arguments became more and more heated, finally turning into slanging matches which only ended when Bruce took refuge in his work.

That, at least, was how I read the situation.

Bruce had plenty of work. His new play was due to go into rehearsal very soon, and there were auditions to be held, and conferences with the director and the management. Pippa was disappointed to have only me to help her make the arrangements for her party, and she blamed me, not his work and not Mandy, for Bruce's absence. For the first time, and to my shocked dismay, I became aware in her of something more than dislike for me. I now felt a real and urgent animosity.

I had been unable to persuade the Greater London Council to let me put up a marquee in the Square for dancing, which Pippa had passionately wanted. As they very reasonably pointed out, the other residents would be disturbed by the noise. So I gained permission, instead, to have one in the long narrow garden behind the house, explaining that our neighbours were coming to the party. This made Pippa sulk. Bruce wouldn't help her against the GLC – he said he hadn't the time – and Mandy didn't care; so Pippa gave me hell. In a way I could understand it. In her eyes it was she and Bruce who were lovers – and it was her twenty-first birthday – and Bruce was taking no interest.

She was convinced that there wouldn't be enough room for all our guests without a marquee. We had invited two hundred and twenty people but I pointed out that, with the tent for the buffet supper and later for breakfast, with the double drawing room for dancing, the morning room for sitting out, and a disco for the younger set in the basement, there would be plenty of room for everyone. She wouldn't be comforted. I realised that she was arguing for the sake of arguing; to demonstrate that I was being unreasonable, and that she was a martyr. Again no one took any notice of her and especially not Bruce. She turned on me – and not unnaturally it completely took away the fun for me in making the preparations.

Another major bone of contention was that, as my play was still running, I would be absent from the early stages of the party. Although the child of a playwright and an actress, Pippa was indifferent to the theatre, and impatient of its disciplines.

'I don't believe you couldn't get a night off, if you really wanted to, Mummy,' she said petulantly. 'After all, I'm only going to be twenty-one once. What are my friends going to think?'

'Don't be silly, darling,' I replied. 'Everyone is only twenty-one once, and the only actress I've ever heard of being given a night off, except for illness, was Gladys Cooper on her eightieth birthday.'

I don't know who told Pippa about Bruce and Mandy quarrelling – Mandy presumably – but when she heard she took it very seriously. She became alarmed that Bruce might cool toward Mandy, and perhaps turn back again to me. He told me years later that she had already made great play of my impending visit to Philip, rousing him time and again to hostility, when she thought he was becoming calmer on the subject.

She really worried about Mandy, and seeing it, Bruce worried too, but not for the reason Pippa hoped. His great love for his daughter was such a habit that nothing by this time could kill it, but he did become alarmed by the venom in her voice when she talked about me. Her excessive jealousy of me hadn't hit him before, perhaps because she had never been so blatant in her expression of it, or perhaps because she had seemed to him too perfect to indulge in such emotions. Now at last he took her to task about it.

She seemed astonished by his reprimand. She vowed she loved me more than anyone except him, but she couldn't help loving him best of all, could she? She said she was upset because the timing of my forthcoming visit to Philip was unkind to both of them, even if Mary *was* dying, since Bruce had this most important play to launch, and she, Pippa, had so wanted this particular dance to be unclouded by family troubles. She said she had only urged Mandy's case because she thought Mandy would be so good for him, as obviously I had ceased to care for him. She said she was only trying to be helpful; that she didn't want him to upset Mandy so much that his whole life with a beautiful girl who loved him, who could make him happy at last, might be put at risk. She was innocence itself, and she would have fooled him except that she couldn't keep her hatred for me out of her voice. She said that she wasn't wanting him to get shot of me except for his own sake and mine. I could take care of myself; and besides, since I didn't care for him, I couldn't be hurt. I had my career and my friends and an impregnable independence, she said; but he had his future to think of. It was all very plausible, but he suddenly realised that he didn't believe a word of it. The whole thing rang false. His beautiful, perfect daughter was telling him a pack of lies, and it made him sick.

When Pippa saw that he disbelieved her, she became coldly angry. Bruce resolved to treat what she said in future with considerable caution, and Pippa decided to take her revenge.

The revenge she chose was entirely effective.

CHAPTER TEN

Until this time, the nearest Bruce and I had come to parting was, as usual, due to my obsession with Philip. Fourteen years before, during the very hot summer of 1966, Bruce had had to go to America for three months, and I had behaved foolishly even by my abysmal standards.

Bruce had had a play done by one of the fringe theatres in London, an American director had seen it, and wanted to direct it himself, off Broadway, if Bruce would make a few changes for the American market. Simultaneously MGM had shown interest in one of his short stories, and were thinking of turning it into a film, and at the same time a request had come via his American agent for him to do a short lecture tour in the States on one of the women's club circuits. Bruce was delighted. I was acting in London, which was becoming more or less usual in those days, and couldn't accompany him, so Pippa (by now a sophisticated six-year-old) and I were left at home.

I missed him very much. In our eight years of marriage I had grown to depend on him, probably more than I should. We were endlessly compatible, and in fact we more or less lived in each other's pockets, so when he went, he left a considerable blank.

I hadn't thought about Philip for years, and I certainly had no desire to see him, so that it was sheer bad luck that I happened to run into him not long after Bruce had gone. Philip was also acting in London, but in another play, and by chance we were both asked to the same after-show supper party. I'd had a matinée and evening show that day and happened to be very tired, but that does not excuse what occurred.

Philip was already there by the time I arrived, and seemed in high spirits and, as ever, surrounded by girls. No one had warned me that he had been invited, so it was a tremendous shock to see him. He was entirely unchanged and that, too, was a shock. I suppose I had hoped, for my own peace of mind, that he would have aged, and in ageing would have lost the power to attract me, but he had not.

Evidently he hadn't been told that I was to be at the party either, because I saw him registering the surprise of my arrival by a slight widening of the eyes, and a tautening of the muscles round his jaw, and I was reminded immediately of what a secretive man he was. How often had I seen him when confronted by the unexpected or unpleasant, registering his discomfort in a similarly guarded way! I suppose as a firmly married man habitually on the prowl he had had many occasions that must have proved difficult to handle.

I pulled myself together as quickly as I could (although I had a moment of faintness which alarmed me), smiled at him vaguely, and waved. He nodded in my direction, then bent his head towards the nearest girl and whispered something to her which made her laugh. I felt myself flushing and self-consciously told my hostess that I was starving. 'Of course, darling!' she breathed ecstatically. 'You must be! So sweet of you to come! Everyone is dying to meet you, but I won't introduce you to a soul until you've had something to eat!' To my relief she didn't seem to have noticed my discomfort and led me to a table groaning with goodies. 'Help yourself,' she said. 'You must be exhausted after such a long part. Pile all you want on a plate, and Malcolm will get you a drink. Oh! Someone else has arrived,' and she darted to the door again all smiles and waving arms, the smell of her heavy scent billowing around her.

Malcolm, who was tall, slim and devastatingly good-looking in a very orthodox way, inched his way towards me, smiling a slow sexy smile. 'Charmed Miss Tracy!' he said. 'What'll it be?' He lowered his voice as though all London could hear and went on, 'I can't recommend the vinegar that passes for wine here, I'm afraid, so why not make it a vodka, what?' He smiled that smile again, and I realised that he thought it was a passport to my heart.

'I don't want the hard stuff at this time of night,' I laughed back politely, 'so it will have to be vinegar, I'm afraid. I'm too tired for no alcohol at a shindig like this.'

'Shindig! Shindig!' he echoed as though relishing the word. 'What a perfect description! We'll have to see more of one another, won't we? Stay right there, and I'll be back in a trice.'

Oh God! I thought. How am I going to get out of this lot?

I obviously couldn't leave at once, so I helped myself to the food as I had been told, and looked round the room for familiar faces. There didn't seem to be any, except Philip's. Worse and worse. The noise had passed the pain barrier, and now someone was turning on the music. Loud. Why had I ever come? Because I was lonely without Bruce ...

Malcolm was back with my drink far too soon – a huge tumbler filled with red wine. 'Sorry!' he said. 'No proper glasses. Only these. But then I suppose you're used to this sort of thing, being an actress.'

'Used to what sort of thing?' I asked coldly, hating him irrationally.

'This sort of party,' he replied, looking surprised. 'Poor man's jet set.'

He had bored me on sight. I'd put him down as vain and probably pompous. Now I added rudeness to his list of defects. 'Why should you think this is a theatrical kind of party?' I asked. 'I can't see anyone I know here. Not one.'

'Oh, well you know how it is. Everyone screaming, extraordinary clothes, and thick tumblers for the drinks.'

I took a swig, and decided I couldn't shout all the insults I'd suddenly like to fling at him, so I sat down and began to eat.

He sat down beside me, and gazed at me, then put a hand on my knee. 'Did you know you're very beautiful?' he yelled, against the music.

'Yes,' I said shortly.

He suddenly laughed. 'Oh, I say,' he said. 'That's most frightfully good, what? I don't go to the theatre much, but I'm sure you're damned amusing in your play.' (I was currently playing Nora in Ibsen's *A Doll's House*!)

I didn't reply, so he said, 'Look here, I don't know anyone here either, so let's make a night of it. Eat up, and then you can lend us your body for the shuffle, what? I can't wait to get my arms round that waist of yours.'

For a moment I didn't understand him, then I realised he wanted me to dance. Well why not? It was a way of avoiding coming face to face with Philip. And after the dance I could slip away and go home. I would have done my duty.

'Well? What do you say?' urged Malcolm.

'I say yes,' I said firmly.

I finished what I had on my plate, and for good measure finished my tumbler of red wine, then added, 'Get me another of these first, though, will you? I need it.'

He looked both wary and disapproving. 'Sure you can take it on board?' he asked doubtfully.

'If you mean will I get drunk, the answer is no I won't, and if you're suggesting do I make a habit of drink, the answer is no I don't. OK?'

'OK,' he said, but I could see he didn't like it. 'But I say, steady on, old girl. No offence meant and all that.'

'No offence taken,' I replied.

74

Malcolm went off obediently to get the drink, and I felt someone coming towards me. He stopped in front of me, and before I looked up I knew that it was Philip.

'You're looking marvellous!' he said. 'Better than ever. Come and dance.'

'I can't,' I said. 'Someone called Malcolm is getting me a drink and I've promised to dance with him.'

'Who's Malcolm?' he asked. 'And where's Bruce?'

'Bruce is in America, on business, and I've no idea who Malcolm is. I've only just met him.'

'Then don't bother about him,' said Philip. 'We haven't seen each other for years. Don't let's waste the opportunity.'

'Whose fault is it that we haven't met for years?' I asked belligerently.

Philip studied me calmly, then said, 'It's the way life goes.'

Before I could answer, Malcolm was back. He seemed annoyed to see Philip, and said, 'Your drink, Miss Tracy,' ignoring him and stretching his arm in front of him with the wine.

'Buzz off,' said Philip. 'June and I are old friends. I've known her since she was a child. I even taught her at drama school.'

'Is that true?' asked Malcolm.

'Yes,' I said. 'Quite true.'

'You said you'd have this dance.'

'Later,' said Philip impatiently. 'She'll dance with you later. We haven't seen each other for years, I told you, and we want to catch up on the news.'

'But you said ...' began Malcolm.

'Beat it,' said Philip. 'Get lost.' He sounded angry.

Malcolm looked down at him. He was at least half a head taller, and probably the stronger, but he was in a dinner jacket which Philip wasn't, and Philip was obviously in good physical shape. What's more he looked as if he meant business. 'OK. If that's how you want it,' he said, 'I'll go.' He

75

glared at Philip who took no notice, smiled stiffly at me, gave a curious formal bow and was gone.

'That's better!' said Philip. He was still standing in front of me.

I took quite a large swig of drink and felt it going at once to my head. Let it, I thought. What does it matter?

Philip said, 'Where do you live now?'

'Just off the King's Road.'

'Splendid!' he said. 'I've taken a temporary lease on a flat near the King's Road too, so we're neighbours.'

I said nothing.

Philip continued, 'I don't know what you think of this party, I think it's crap. Why don't we go to your place for old time's sake?'

'No thanks. Besides my daughter Pippa is there, not to mention the au pair.'

'OK,' he replied cheerfully, 'then come to my pad.'

'No thanks,' I repeated. 'I'm through with all that.'

'Not pleased to see me?'

'Not very.'

'Why not? We're friends.'

'I'm glad you think so.'

'Well of course I do! We've had good times together.'

'Look,' I said, 'I'm married now.'

'So?'

'And I love my husband.'

He considered this, then said, 'So?'

'So it's no thanks,' I said, and I finished the drink, which was a mistake.

Philip didn't reply for a moment or two, but he watched me closely, then murmured into a lull in that fantastic noise, 'It seems a pity to part as enemies. I thought you understood how it was with Mary and me.'

'I thought you knew how it was with me,' I retorted.

'In my book,' he said, 'I'm married, and I'm not going to

76

get unmarried. You know the form. But if Mary is away, and Bruce isn't about, it's not as though we're strangers, so why not make the best of it?'

'You're quite something!' I exclaimed indignantly, but even through the waves of drink I could hear the self-pity in my voice. 'You drop me for years, then calmly come back and say let's start up all over again.'

'That's it,' he said encouragingly.

'Well you know what I think,' I said firmly.

'That's just it. I don't. I know what you say, which isn't at all the same thing.'

The drink was really having its effect now. 'No, no, no, no, no,' I said, shaking my head, but my voice was slurring, and Philip heard it. 'No, no, no, because I love Bruce.'

'Yes, yes, yes, yes, yes,' he answered smiling. 'Yes, my wonderful darling. We're going to make love again, and my God how I've missed you!'

My foolish unquenchable heart leapt at this, but I still shook my fuddled head. 'There's Bruce,' I said obstinately.

'I know,' he said softly, 'but he's an ocean and miles away, and you'll never get over me. I'm in your bloodstream, just as you are in mine. You love me, my darling, and you always will.'

Yes, I thought helplessly. I love you and I always will, but I love Bruce too, and it's too late for you and me.

He pulled me up out of the chair, and kissed me long and hard on the lips, and all over again I was drowned in love for him.

'Oh, Philip,' I said foolishly.

'Oh, June,' he echoed, his mouth very close to my ear. 'Come on,' he continued, 'we're getting out of here. Where's your coat?'

'The maid took it by the front door when I came in.'

'Right. Have you got a car?'

'Yes.'

77

'Good. You're in no state to drive, so I'll do the driving.'

'I'm not drunk,' I protested.

'You could have fooled me,' he answered.

The cold air hit me, and I clutched Philip for support. He laughed exultantly. 'That's my girl,' he said. 'We're going to have a wonderful time.'

I gave him the car keys, and leaning my head against his shoulder, I went to sleep. The last thing I remember before I slept was thinking, 'I'm home at last.'

CHAPTER ELEVEN

Even though I struggled and protested when he undressed me and we lay on the bed, I didn't struggle hard, and I didn't protest as though I meant it. I am ashamed of myself, and there is no excuse. No excuse at all. It was stupid on my own account, and cruel to Bruce, but of course I was happy. Wildly, desperately, wickedly, utterly happy. I didn't stop to think that a great measure of my happiness came from being able to kid myself that Philip hadn't rejected me after all; that still after all these years he wanted me, as he had always wanted me. And how had he always wanted me? Physically. The way he had wanted dozens of other women. There's no fool like a woman in love! I did stop to think of Bruce, but it didn't protect me from my old demon, my love for Philip.

We made love all night long, and when I went to sleep at last as the sun was shining in through the windows, he was watching me closely as I lay supine in his arms. He woke me at noon and made love to me again, then woke me again to say that he had telephoned my home and told them not to worry; that I should be home after the show that night. He had remembered to send my love to Pippa, and to say I would be bringing her a present, and he had fobbed off the au pair's curiosity by saying that I was staying with a school friend in trouble.

'Some school friend,' I said anxiously. 'I went to a girls' school!'

'Don't worry,' he said. 'We can polish up the story later. Come on. Love me.'

'I can't!' I exclaimed. 'I'm dead. I've got a hangover and a headache, and I feel terrible.'

'One more time,' he said. 'Then we'd better get some food and go to our theatres.'

'I've only got a party dress here.'

'So tell them at the theatre you're going out again tonight.'

'And what on earth shall I do about my face, and all the smeared make-up?'

'Later,' he said. 'We'll deal with that later. Love now. Do as you're told and like it.'

He rolled on top of me, and splayed out my arms. 'I like you like this!' he said. 'Helpless and in a mess and feeling lousy but obedient. It's a different you, and it appeals. Oh yes, it appeals.'

'But . . .'

'Try *not* to love me then,' he said, 'because I'm going to make love to you. Try not to!' I didn't, and it was magic.

Hey ho! The idiot girl who couldn't learn her lesson!

When I got back home everything was quiet. Pippa was asleep and Nanette, the au pair, had gone to bed. They asked surprisingly few questions in the morning. The following day, Philip called on us. From the start he made a great fuss of both Pippa and the au pair, and presently they got into the habit of seeing him around; they took it for granted that I would be seeing him after the show most nights. He knew how to deal with women of all ages. My God he did! They fell like all the rest.

It was all too good to last, of course, but no one, even me at my most pessimistic, could have foreseen the melodramatic climax that would shatter my stolen happiness.

I knew Bruce was still in America because he rang me every other day, so I was safe from him. Philip and I always

80

used his flat and there was no danger of us being caught there, as Mary was in Suffolk and never moved without telling him; besides, I noticed that he telephoned her without fail, once a day. However, he had been making a play for a girl in his company – as I should have known – and she grew suspicious because he had cooled towards her all of a sudden. In her jealousy she had taken to watching him. She had therefore seen, without either of us having the slightest suspicion, that Philip and I were at his flat most nights after the show, and that he spent day after day at my house.

Apparently she had thought of surprising us at Philip's place and making some sort of scene, probably threatening to tell his wife, but when she hinted at the theatre that she knew about me, Philip had become angry and, to stop her gossiping, had been so rude to her that she went completely crazy.

Her father, who was a retired army officer, had a pistol – to deal with burglars apparently – and one night she decided to follow us to Philip's flat, gun in hand. Unfortunately, or perhaps fortunately, we didn't go to his flat. We had a sedate little dinner at home, with the au pair hovering happily round us. Philip left early – the time must have been about half past eleven. I saw him off at the door, and as I turned to go upstairs, I heard a sharp bang. I didn't recognise it as a pistol shot, but the shout which followed it made me vaguely uneasy. A few minutes later the front door bell rang, and Nanette went to answer it. She came to me babbling with fright, and so incoherent that I couldn't understand a word she was saying. I begged her to speak slower.

'It is Monsieur, Monsieur!' she cried hysterically. ''E is covered wis blood, and 'e is dying! Oh 'e look so pale! So awful! I cannot bear it!' She burst into tears. 'There are many people downstairs, Madame, and I don't know what to do! You must come, Madame! You must come quickly!'

I raced downstairs to the hall to find all hell breaking loose.

81

Philip had been put into one of the hall chairs. He looked deathly pale and there was blood pouring from a wound in his shoulder. He had only been nicked, nothing serious, but the blood made it look bad. Three other people were in the hall – the two young men who had found him (one of whom was, by a miracle, a doctor) and a large fat woman with greedy eyes raking in all the details in the hopes of scandal.

'I brought him here,' she said, excitedly but with enormous satisfaction. 'I do hope I did the right thing, Miss Tracy, but I happened to see him coming out of your house, then I saw a sort of flash, and he fell down just under a street lamp, and I saw a girl running away. It's Mr Goodson, isn't it? I recognised him at once, and I recognise you too. I've always admired you. And it's lovely to meet you. You see, as I said, I saw him coming from here.'

'Yes, thank you,' I said, cursing her under my breath. 'You certainly did the right thing. He had been dining here after the show. Thank you so much.'

One of the young men spoke. 'May I use your phone to ring the police?' he asked.

I nodded anxiously. The situation was becoming worse and worse. The fat woman was right to look gleeful.

'Of course,' I said. 'What shall we do with Mr Goodson? Should he go to hospital?'

'No. He'll be all right,' said the doctor, 'but perhaps we could make him a little more comfortable for the questioning. Is there a sofa somewhere?'

I led the way, and the two men supported him up the stairs to the drawing room on the first floor. The fat woman followed us, braying her excitement. I couldn't get rid of her, as the police would want to question her too. Nanette, still hysterical, hovered around, and Pippa ran down from her bedroom. When she saw Philip, she burst into tears. Although she was genuinely upset she added her own sense of drama, which impressed the others, and annoyed me. I did my best to comfort her, then sent her back to bed with Nanette to look after her.

It was two o'clock before the police had finished their questions and the house was quiet again.

Next day, it was in all the papers – thanks, no doubt, to our fat friend. There were photographs of Philip, me, and the fat woman (whose name was Mrs Bracegirdle, which somehow made everything grimly ludicrous). Bruce heard about it in America, and flew back at once. The peace of our marriage was ended for good.

What made Pippa realise so completely that it was I who was at fault about the whole business? It was the school holidays, so she wouldn't have been hearing gossip. Bruce and I went to great pains, in spite of our distress, to keep up appearances in front of her, and Nanette appeared to have seen nothing wrong in our relationship. And yet at six years old, when one wouldn't have thought an affair like this would have been noticed let alone been interesting to her, Pippa knew as if by radar that Philip and I had sinned, and that Bruce was the innocent party. In an uncannily adult way, she offered Bruce solace and her undying loyalty, and I was right out in the cold. Pippa and Bruce were the family. I was the eternal outsider.

Pippa, dainty in her frilly little dresses, became the woman of the household, and I wasn't even as close to her as Nanette. I was a non-person to her, and Bruce went along with it. He had been too hurt to protect me, and was too besotted by Pippa to see how unnatural her behaviour was.

It was Pippa's first real victory, and my total defeat.

Philip, meantime, recovered quickly from the superficial flesh wound and Mary welcomed him back with relief and satisfaction. For her, as well as for Pippa, it was an important victory. As a news story, however, it remained hovering in the air for longer than most of its kind. The case didn't come to court for several months. When it did, the girl got an eighteen-month prison sentence for attempted murder. When she was released, with time off for custody and good behaviour, she gave the media a field day.

CHAPTER TWELVE

What an evening Pippa's party turned out to be!

The preliminaries could not have gone more smoothly. The marquee in the garden looked festive with its fairy lights and massed hydrangeas, and even though I had to leave for my performance long before the first guest was due, it was obvious that the caterers had done a splendid job. The little band were old friends and excellent musicians, too, so all in all I felt I had done the best I could as an absentee hostess.

I have never seen Pippa look more beautiful. She had an inner excitement (which I recognised, but didn't understand until later) which gave her beauty an extra dimension. Her usually pale cheeks were flushed and her great eyes sparkled with anticipation. Bruce, of course, looked his handsome solid self.

When I returned, the party was in full swing and I received many compliments from our guests. But I felt apprehensive for some reason. The dark red dress which I had bought for the occasion, and which had cost a fortune, suddenly hadn't suited me when I put it on at the theatre (an opinion depressingly shared by Nellie, my dresser): Mandy, at her prettiest in clouds of yellow chiffon, did nothing to raise my spirits.

Pippa's boyfriends had turned up in force, and she was in demand for every dance. I had my work cut out as the hostess. Bruce, once he had done his duty, danced the night away with Mandy and her young friends in the disco in the basement. All went well until almost the end, when I saw Mandy and Bruce having a heated argument. Mandy left the house in tears, and Bruce then collected everyone together in the drawing room to make a birthday speech for Pippa. It was a good speech: funny and appropriate and it went down well. Then it was Pippa's turn to reply.

She thanked Bruce very sweetly for what he had said. She thanked us both politely for the party. She thanked all the guests for coming. And then she sprang her surprise.

'I'm twenty-one today,' she smiled. 'I have the key of the door. But my dear friends, I shan't need it. You are the first to know. I haven't even told my beloved father and mother yet. Charles Pilkington and I are engaged. Charles asked me to marry him tonight, and I have said yes. I know my parents like him. Had I been younger, he might have had to ask my father's permission: I know my father would have given it.' I glanced across at Bruce, who was looking white and shocked. 'But we didn't need to ask him. Instead I'm giving Daddy and everyone else here tonight this lovely surprise. Ladies and gentlemen, I ask you to charge your glasses, to wish Charles and me health and happiness. Thank you.'

And demurely she left the little dais and walked over to Charles, and in front of us all they kissed.

There was a hubbub of surprise, congratulations and laughter, everyone waving their glasses in drunken euphoria or genuine delight. Finally someone shouted for a speech from Charles. Bruce was literally trembling with shock, and I confess that I felt dazed.

Charles looked almost as winded and shaken as Bruce and I, but he is a poised and civilised person, whom indeed we both liked, and if a speech was demanded of him, a speech he would give.

Charles is a well-scrubbed, elegantly casual young man,

with straight dark hair, a large lock of which is inclined to fall over his forehead. His manners and breeding are impeccable. He has a good job in export-import, and as a son-in-law he was all we might wish for except that we had no idea that Pippa even liked him. If she had fallen in love with him, it had been very sudden indeed – although that is always possible. We knew that he was keen on Pippa, because he had been hanging around for some time.

He spoke clearly and kindly, but he was evidently embarrassed by the situation, having seen how upset Bruce was – and this at least demonstrated his sensitivity, a quality totally absent at that moment in our daughter. Her mouth was a little open as she watched her new fiancé speak and her eyes shone with satisfaction. I didn't understand at the time why she was so delighted to have sprung this particular surprise at her party. Later I was to realise how important it was to be for us all.

Charles announced that he had never been happier, and that he now – even if late – asked Bruce's permission to marry his daughter. He promised to take care of Pippa, and to work for her and love her all his days. I felt deeply grateful to him for showing so clearly that he cared for us all, and hoped Bruce felt something of my emotion; but I knew that he was too bitterly hurt to take aboard any other feelings.

When Charles came off the little platform he came towards Bruce and me awkwardly.

'I hope you don't mind too much. It must be a tremendous shock.'

He didn't apologise, and I understood he was taking the entire blame for their decision on himself. As I was sure that the idea had been Pippa's, I admired him for this too, and hoped that Pippa would be good to him.

The party went on its way, Bruce made himself scarce, Pippa and Charles danced together for the rest of the evening, and I tried to go on being the perfect hostess. Things ground to a halt at around five in the morning, and Bruce was nowhere to be seen for the goodbyes.

As Pippa and I went up the stairs together, she slipped her arm through mine. It was all I could do not to disengage myself; I had seldom felt angrier. Pippa must have known what I felt. She is no fool, but she elected to pretend that I was as pleased as she was at how things had gone; that we were girls together, and wanted nothing better than a girlish chat. I went along with it, because I was curious to know a little more of what was going on in her devious mind. We went into the drawing room, kicked off our shoes, lay back on one of the sofas and talked – or rather Pippa did.

'Gosh, I'm so excited, darling!' she exclaimed. 'I've always been mad about Charles, but I never dreamed he cared for me!' As he had been mooning around for some two years I found this hard to swallow. 'Isn't it wonderful?' she went on. 'I'm to meet his parents at the weekend – they live in Yorkshire – and we want to be married in about three months' time. Huge wedding, if you and Daddy don't mind, and if it's not too expensive after this wonderful party. We want to ask everyone, and have bridesmaids and pages, and an enormous reception and a honeymoon in the Caribbean. Then we're going to look for a little place in Chelsea, not too far from here, and we're going to have a house in Wiltshire for the weekends, which you and Daddy can come to as often as you like. Isn't it all divine? Aren't I lucky? Won't everyone be jealous?'

This last sentence hung in the air between us, and after a moment or two she added, 'Not that I want anyone to be jealous, of course!'

I wondered where Bruce was, and why Pippa was having this particular conversation without him. She seemed to sense this.

'Where's Daddy, d'you know?'

'He disappeared some time ago,' I said. 'I think it made

him rather unhappy that you hadn't told him anything before you announced your engagement. You know how much he loves you – and he had to hear about it in front of a crowd. Not quite the way he would have wished, probably.'

'I just couldn't keep the news to myself,' she cooed. 'I'm sure he'll realise that, when he's had time to think. You didn't mind, did you?' She looked me square in the face, and she had drawn her mouth into a thin line.

'I minded about the way you did it,' I said. 'Very much.'

This seemed to surprise her, and she said rather lamely, 'Well, you know how it is.'

'Anyway,' I said, 'I hope you'll be very happy. Take care of Charles, won't you? He's rather special, I think.'

This seemed to annoy her, but she covered up her annoyance, and said, 'I'm mad about the boy, I tell you. I'll be the perfect wife.'

'I hope so,' I answered drily. I didn't mean to say it, but it was out before I could stop it.

She yawned colossally and said, 'My, my, I'm dead, aren't you? Beddy-byes, Mummy. It's after six.'

So we went to our bedrooms, arm in arm.

Bruce was already asleep, and I was thankful. Quite enough for him to deal with tomorrow.

I didn't sleep a wink, and I was right to have been so disturbed.

CHAPTER THIRTEEN

Between the shooting incident and Pippa's party, I had worked with Philip once again, in a three-months' run of a bad play in the West End.

When I heard that he was to be one of the cast, I wasn't at all keen. Until the shooting we had always managed to conduct our affair without a scandal; so when one broke, I felt smirched, and the affair suddenly seemed squalid. All affairs are fundamentally squalid, I suppose, as indeed are the mechanisms of sex! It's that old magician, Imagination, which turns them into the great love, the great excitement, the panacea for all ills. This is why, without it, boredom often goes hand in hand with sexual euphoria. At any rate, I hadn't been proud of Philip or myself when we were found out, and I didn't try to get in touch with him afterwards.

When I was offered the play with him, I asked Bruce whether he would prefer me not to do it. I had known all along that Philip was not a good actor, but I had firmly shut my eyes to it. He had been my tutor, after all, as well as the love of my life. I had suspected even from the first that no really confident actor teaches at drama school, and when I had acted with him in South Africa, even at the height of my love for him, I had secretly wished he was better in the play. Now, without love to sustain me, and a play in which I had little faith, was it worth the effort of being with him? Bruce said yes. Why, now that I look back on it, I'm not sure. Perhaps he thought that acting in a flop with

Philip might cure me of my obsession. If so, he was right.

To begin with, Philip had changed enough to lose his attraction for me at long last. He was definitely ageing. His hair had gone grey and he had a permanent stoop. The chip on his shoulder was now also too evident to be endearing – if indeed it ever had been. I found him difficult to be with in a company. He hated the leading man for obvious reasons, and showed it. He was a lazy actor who not only didn't learn his lines properly, but ad-libbed embarrassingly when found out; and he was instinctively anti-management, and so liable to make trouble among the small fry. All the same, after so long I couldn't ignore him, and he insisted on spending a good deal of time in my company.

Nothing in the world is more completely dead than a dead love affair, but Philip was so used to my uncritical adoration that he seemed unable to believe that things were or could be different. He naturally flirted with the plainest girl in the cast, who even at his present age fell for him with the usual resulting tears and scenes – so he had no idea that his charms had faded.

The difference in our relationship this time was that he was now keener than I to pick up where we had left off. Always before he had avoided kissing my lips if he could help it, unless it was a necessary lead-up to seduction. Like telling me that he loved me, this seemed to be more than he wished to give away. Now he did both, and he lay in wait for me to take me to lunch or to see me home after the show. At any time previously I would have been in seventh heaven. Now I wanted none of it. He was possessive in front of the rest of the company, and indeed in front of the director, which I disliked, and I couldn't shake him off.

I knew unswervingly that I must use this time to bury my love for him so deep that it could never rise again to haunt me and spoil the rest of my life. With this end in view, I was frank with him, but I hope not unnecessarily cruel. I told him I was out of love with him, and that the affair was over at last: he refused to believe me. He suddenly began telling hard-luck stories of his childhood – presumably to win my sympathy (too late). When he turned to boasting of his conquests I looked as bored as I felt. When he gossiped about the others in the cast, I told him I hated gossip. Previously he would have left me at once had I behaved in such a manner: now he stayed by me, and for once I was not available.

Robert Fellows, the leading man, had taken to me, and I enjoyed his company. Bruce, too, came to see me often, with friends with whom we dined after the show. My dressing room became as crowded as Waterloo Station – which Philip hated. Throughout the run I watched Philip and analysed him, with a detachment quite new in our relationship; and I found him, when weighed in the balance, gravely wanting. Had I known all there was to know, I might have been less harsh. As it was, I was able to free myself from him completely. The time wasted with him had been too long.

I had a recurring dream at this period – a dream that was so insistent and so regular that I came to dread it.

I had been looking for Philip's house, wandering lost and anxious in wooded countryside. Suddenly I saw a cottage that I knew by instinct was his. I went to the front door, and rang the bell. I heard it pealing loudly through the little house, then Philip himself came to the door. I had expected him to be angry, but he was all smiles, and looked very handsome and very young. He led me through to a small sitting room where Mary was seated in a winged armchair in front of a blazing log fire, knitting. She too was all smiles. Philip introduced her to me formally, then he and I went out into the garden at the back of the cottage, which he told me he very specially wanted me to see. There were no flowers, indeed no flower beds. We found ourselves in a small square plot, penned in by high staked-fences, and the ground had been tarred over – hard and blue-black. There was nothing

92

whatever in the plot – not a shrub, a blade of grass, a small statue, or a weed. Nothing at all. When I turned to Philip for an explanation, he wasn't there – and then I woke up.

The bleakness of that empty garden haunted me.

I had my birthday during this engagement. In all the long years, Philip had never bothered to ask me my age or the date of my birth (I knew his, and had treasured them). I told him now that Bruce and I would be celebrating mine the next day, and on the following evening he gave me a little package. When I opened it, I found a small, carefully crayonned picture of a naked woman with heavy breasts, large hips, and scarlet pubic hair; the picture was signed by himself. After I had thanked him for it and he had left the room, I tore it up and dropped it with disgust into the waste-paper basket.

Our last day together I shall never forget. Even he must have realised by this time that I felt very little for him any more, so with some determination he had come to my room to try to make things better before we parted. He had a strangely heavy tread for such a small man, and a very Wagnerian way of knocking on the door. He came between the matinée and evening shows on the last Saturday, and I was resting on my divan, dressed in a frilly pink dressing gown.

'Pretty,' he said approvingly when he saw me, although he had seen me in that garment dozens of times and more. 'Pink suits you.'

In order to get to sleep between shows I had turned out most of the lights, and in the semi-darkness he looked young ... almost boyish.

He sat by my feet on the divan. 'Hope I'm not interrupting you,' he said, heartily.

'Of course not,' I replied politely.

93

'We don't seem to have seen so much of each other, this time.'

'No,' I agreed.

'Of course, you've got your usual huge part, and I my usual small one, so our dressing rooms have been miles apart.'

'Yes,' I said, apologetically.

'I'm quite proud of the fact that I taught you to act,' he said. 'I boast about it.'

This genuinely touched me, and I thanked him.

'I'm proud of the fact that I taught you to make love, too,' he said. 'But I don't boast about that.' He laughed.

'No.' I laughed too, but for the first time I wondered if he did. Not at first, of course, when it might have made things difficult with Mary – but lately. Then I disliked myself for entertaining the idea, although it still persisted.

'Have you ever told anyone? Mary? The latest girlfriend?' I asked.

He looked away from me and blustered, 'What do you take me for?'

I knew then that he had, and wondered how often, and to whom, and the thought gave me the same feeling of having been smirched as when we had had our names blazoned on the front pages of the newspapers, after the shooting. Silly, I thought, and dishonest too, only to feel unclean when I'm found out. What had poor Bruce felt? And what was he feeling now, even though it had been he who had suggested I do the play?

Philip suddenly dived forward and kissed me hard on the mouth. I struggled, but he took no notice and began to caress me.

'Don't,' I said. 'I don't want it.'

He ignored me.

'Get out!' I said angrily. 'Get out, and stay out!'

'Oh, come on,' he laughed. 'It's a bit late to play the prim virgin!'

94

'Get out,' I repeated, 'or I'll scream the place down!'

'You do that very thing and see what happens,' he said confidently, and he laughed again.

I opened my mouth to scream and he suddenly lost his temper. He hit me hard across the cheek; so hard that I thought my jaw was broken. Then he put his hands round my throat and shook my head until I thought my neck would break.

'Little snob!' he said, with a world of contempt in his voice. 'Forget your old friends, and only have it off with the new and successful. It's Robert who turns you on now, isn't it? You're a tramp – but you know that – I don't know why I bothered.'

I was panting heavily, and so scared that I couldn't speak.

He got up off the sofa, looked at me with loathing and spat in my face. Shocked I began scrubbing my face with a handkerchief, twisting my head from side to side.

'Tramp! Whore!' he yelled. 'I'll never forgive you for this afternoon. Never!' He spat at me again, then turned to go. At the door he said, 'Doesn't Bruce mind that you're a tramp? Poor weak sod, I suppose he's still in love with you!'

When he had gone I was so horrified that I burst into tears. Afterwards, when I had pulled myself together, I telephoned Bruce. He was surprised to hear me, and evidently divined that I was upset, although I was trying to hide it.

'What's up?' he asked.

'Nothing really,' I replied, 'except that tonight is our last performance, and I wanted you to know that I'm glad that I'll be more at home.'

'D'you want me to be there?' he asked. 'Because I will if you like.'

'Don't bother,' I said. 'There'll be all the goodbyes and the packing up and so on, but I'll be delighted to be out of work tomorrow, and I wanted you to know that.'

'Fine,' he said, but he sounded equivocal. 'Fine. It was nice of you to phone!'

The performance went well, but the packing up was as dreary as it always is when a show ends. As Bruce hadn't come to fetch me, Robert and I went to the Ritz for a drink once all the goodbyes were over. Philip passed us in his car on our way in: he gave the V sign and tooted on his horn.

'I don't like that man,' said Robert. 'What's the chip about, d'you know?'

'No,' I said, 'I don't. I've known him a thousand years, but I've never known why he had it.'

And now I was going to see him again, and I wasn't looking forward to it. Yet, against all logic, my imagination had given him the benefit of many doubts and – such is the nature of the disease – had reinstated him as my lost love.

I have always had this curious inner imagination, which lives a submerged but insistent life of its own. It is immensely important to me, but it bears little relation to life as I live it otherwise. And yet it dominates me. Is it some vestigial trace of a life I have lived before, or one that I have yet to live? Why does my recognition of it pacify some inner turbulence? At some time or some place, I know I must give it space: live through it. So I accept its hidden dominance.

PART TWO

The Visit

CHAPTER FOURTEEN

Throughout the entire visit June had the curious surrealist sense of slow motion that one experiences when falling or skidding towards a bad accident. Powerless to save herself, she yet seemed to have all the time in the world to do so. A fair comment, she thought, on the whole of her affair with Philip.

No one saw her off when she left for Suffolk to visit Mary Goodson. Bruce and she were sleeping in different rooms now, but usually they and Pippa met around breakfast-time and, despite the tensions, they did at least talk to one another. Today Pippa and Bruce had stayed away, and June realised how deep was her disgrace. Pippa's defection, surely far more serious than her own, had apparently already been forgiven. It was a brilliant autumn day: mountains of white cumulus sailed lazily across a bright blue sky and a yellow picturebook sun sharpened the colours of the turning leaves.

Although Pippa hadn't come to breakfast, June had seen her just as she was leaving, and the sight had been strangely disquieting. She was already in the car, when she became aware that she was being watched and glanced up at the drawing room window. She saw Pippa, half-hidden behind the curtains, staring down at her with a curious expression – almost it seemed of triumph – on her face. June waved and smiled, but Pippa neither waved nor smiled back; simply glided out of sight. Trying to reassure herself that she was imagining an unpleasantness that wasn't there, June briskly started the car.

She had left a letter for Bruce on the hall table. It had taken her some time to write, and in it she had tried to express her love for him. Not for the first time she bitterly regretted that she had agreed to go to Suffolk, but there was no going back on it now: she had asked his forgiveness for the visit and had tried to give her reasons for her obstinacy. She acknowledged that their marriage was in a bad state, and accepted her share of the blame, but swore that when she returned she would have finished with Philip for good. Her only wish for the future was that Bruce would be happy: if he still needed her, it would give her the greatest happiness to try and make him so. He had been a marvellous husband under extremely trying circumstances, but those circumstances would no longer apply. She told him that she admired him, and respected him, and that her love for him was unchanged.

She wondered how he would take it.

The North Orbital road had not yet been built, so to avoid London's East End June made her way up the Finchley Road and on to the A1. After Hatfield she turned right and was soon passing through Much Hadham. She had never been there, but looked around her with curiosity, knowing that Philip and Mary had lived there for many years. It was a charming village. The old houses huddled together in companionable grace, unchallenged and undiminished by modern buildings; and illogically, when she headed for the wide horizons beyond Stortford, she did so with a lightened heart.

She loved this Essex countryside, with its pargeted town houses, its spiv-shouldered thatched cottages, its sturdy churches, and the vast cornfields drenched in the special light which had so inspired Constable, Cotman and Seago. But as she approached the Suffolk boundary she found her thoughts becoming centred wholly on Philip – and suddenly remembered with a daunting clarity her last time with him at the theatre. In her mind's eye she saw his face disfigured by hatred and rage, and heard his voice blaming her for leading him on. Even after all this time, she shuddered at the recollection.

When she left their house tomorrow, she must indeed sever all connection with him and Mary, and live without their shadows in her life. How often she had been resolved on this, and failed! But this time she must succeed. In her obsession with Philip she had continually abandoned reality in exchange for the intense demands of her inner world. Her marriage, alas, had been one casualty; and Pippa, another. Never again must the balances be tilted towards her secret life. Reality, which might at first seem impoverishment, if persevered with could only be gain. She sighed.

A large sign on the left of the road proclaimed 'Suffolk': she was nearly at her destination. Her pulse quickened. What would his home be like? Philip had never talked to her about any of his houses, or encouraged her curiosity on the subject; as always, protecting his privacy. Since he had been so completely the dominant partner in their relationship, it did not occur to her that Mary might be the dominant partner in his.

She lost her way twice, and by the time she reached the village of Berg-Septon she was late. The great wrought-iron gates of an estate with eighteenth-century lodges came up on her left, then she dropped steeply down through the village to a ford which crossed the street and guarded access to the houses climbing the opposing hillside (how typical of Philip, she thought, to have found such a place!). Next came a large lath-and-plaster house decorated with pargetry, called 'Little Choppins', and then at last on the gates of a gravelled driveway, a sign saying 'Choppins'.

The drive was long, and flanked with rhododendrons. Huge old trees reared up behind them, and round a curve in the drive stood a large Regency house, square, uncompromising but well-proportioned.

It was a grey house with grey tiles and dark green shuttered windows; the last sort of house she would have associated with Philip. As so often in their long acquaintance, it threw her. The wide lawn in front of the house ran down to a lake, and the house itself asserted money and the establishment. Had Philip made more money than she had thought, or was Mary rich?

She rang the doorbell, and a uniformed nurse came to the door. 'Ah, Miss Tracy,' she said. 'Come in. Margaret will take you to your room, and Mr Goodson is expecting you in the drawing room.' She stared at June for a moment with what seemed like suppressed hostility, then stepped aside so that she could enter.

The hall was large and light, with a wooden floor and coloured rugs.

'Thank you,' said June. 'How is Mrs Goodson?'

'Tired, but doing wonderfully,' said the nurse warmly. 'She wants to see you for a few minutes before lunch. Then, after she has had her rest, she wants you to have tea with her.'

'Of course,' said June. 'I'm looking forward to seeing her.'

For a moment the nurse looked disapproving, then she said briskly, 'And she looks forward to seeing you, but first Mr Goodson is expecting you.'

A pretty dark-haired girl in her twenties now appeared behind the nurse, who turned to her and said crisply, 'The Blue Room, Margaret.'

'This way,' said the maid. 'I'll take your case.'

They went up the graceful staircase, past large ancestral portraits, to the first landing.

The Blue Room lived up to its name. Blue silk curtains flanked the tall windows. The Hepplewhite four-poster was draped in blue silk and there was a blue and buff silk rug on the powder-blue carpet. A large bathroom opened off the room, with a deep old-fashioned bath with brass taps, and pot pourri in a bowl on a table by the bath. Surprisingly a Picasso lithograph was over the bath, but the pictures in the bedroom were eighteenth- and early nineteenth-century landscapes.

Margaret left her, and June washed her hands and combed her hair before descending the stairs again to find the drawing room. She felt like a naughty girl at school, summoned by her headmistress.

The drawing room had four windows, and like the hall and bedroom was filled with good pictures. It was decorated predominantly in a gentle salmon pink. Great armfuls of flowers were on the various tables. A fire was burning in a Regency grate, and with his back to it stood Philip.

He was an old man now, though it was only five years since she had seen him last. His back was bowed, and his hair quite white. His face was drawn, and he wore a shabby suit. When June came in he seemed hardly to hear her, then he pulled himself together and offered her a drink.

'You're looking well,' he said, 'and very charming as always.'

June smiled nervously. 'I'm so very sorry I'm late,' she said. 'How is she?'

'Marvellous,' he said. 'The courage of a lion.' He shook his head, looked bereft and said, 'Let's see, it was gin, wasn't it?'

In spite of the circumstances June felt shocked that he had forgotten. 'Vodka,' she said. 'If you have it.'

'Ah, yes, vodka. I'm sure we've got some somewhere ... Here we are, vodka – and tonic?'

'Please.' She felt like a stranger.

He gave her a glass and asked if she had had a good drive, then said, 'When you've drunk that we'll go up and see her for a minute or two. OK?'

'Of course. What a lovely house!'

'Yes,' he said. 'Mary's doing. All of it. She has excellent taste, and of course the money, thank God. It pays for her

103

nursing, so she won't have to go away to a nursing home. I couldn't bear that.' He brushed a hand before his eyes, and June saw tears glistening on his eyelashes.

She looked away. 'Have you been here long?' she asked. She felt such a surge of pity for him that her throat ached.

He looked surprised. 'Of course,' he said. 'Sixteen years.'

'Of course,' she replied, dazed. 'How silly of me. You like East Anglia?' she murmured stupidly.

'Mary's home run,' he said. 'Her family come from Suffolk.'

'I see,' she said. There was a pause, then she went on impulsively. 'How are you, yourself? Mary's illness must be such a strain for you.'

Again he looked surprised. 'I'm all right,' he said. 'At least I suppose so. And you?'

'Fine.'

'And Bruce, and the girl?'

'Fine.'

She sat in one of the armchairs, and he sat in another. 'Cheers,' he said, and started humming under his breath.

June tried to think of something to say, and failed, so drank her vodka in silence. Presently the nurse came in. She looked fondly at Philip and said, 'She's ready, sir, when you are.'

'Great!' exclaimed Philip. 'Come on,' he said to June. 'Mary is ready for us.' He made it sound as though it was a treat.

Mary's room was decorated in sea-green. The Italianate bed was enormous, and draped in green and gold. Mary, looking tiny, thin and frail, sat propped against the pillows. All round her and all over the room were flowers, many of them with cards propped up against the vases. Almost like a first night, thought June wryly, and Philip, reading her thoughts as usual, said 'Good-luck messages', and smiled at Mary, who smiled back at him trustingly.

Two chairs had been drawn up by the bed, and June took

104

one, Philip the other. 'Have you had a drink?' asked Mary.

'Yes,' said Philip, 'of course. What do you think I am?' He patted one of his wife's emaciated hands on the coverlet.

'Will you have another?' she asked June. 'We have some up here, don't we, Nurse?'

The nurse smiled possessively. 'Certainly, Madam.' She was young and tall and plain, with pale red hair and small blue eyes. She had a straight back, and moved stiffly.

'No thanks,' said June, and Mary nodded at the nurse.

'Thank you, Nurse, dear,' she said. 'We can manage on our own, now.'

The nurse left the room.

'How lovely of you to come!' exclaimed Mary. 'So good of you. How did the dance go?'

'Fine,' lied June.

'Family well?'

'Very.'

'Working hard?'

'Yes, thank you.'

'How pretty you are!' said Mary. 'She's so pretty, isn't she, Philip?'

'Yes,' said Philip indifferently.

'We're going to have tea together,' said Mary. 'Just you and me. I have to have a rest after lunch but I have so much to say to you.'

'Don't tire yourself,' urged Philip anxiously.

'Of course I won't, but I want to talk to June. I need to.' Mary spoke with surprising strength.

'Of course. Of course.' Philip was placatory.

'It's odd when you're dying,' she continued conversationally. 'There are certain things you want to clear up before you leave. Philip doesn't understand it, but I'm sure you do.'

'Yes,' said June. 'I do.' She hoped she sounded convincing. What, she wondered, did Mary want to 'clear up' with her? Her heart plummeted.

'I hope you'll find your room comfortable.'

'I'm sure I will.'

June was becoming nervous and impatient with this small talk.

'Philip won't be joining us at tea,' said Mary.

'Yes, you told me,' replied June sharply.

Mary looked at her steadily. 'Oh, did I? I'm sorry. I hope you don't mind?'

'Of course not,' said June, feeling ashamed of herself.

'I shall feel so much better when we have talked,' said Mary. 'It will be a great weight off my mind. You've no idea how grateful I am to you for coming. Now, I'm sure you must be hungry. I have asked Cook to make you an especially delicious meal. I hope you will enjoy it. She's a good soul. She has been with us more than twenty years. People stay with us a long time usually. The gardener is the son of the one my parents had, and my secretary has been here fifteen years.'

Secretary? Why on earth a secretary? thought June. The scale on which they evidently lived confused her. Had it always been like this? How little she knew of their circumstances! How completely Philip had guarded himself! Why should Mary need a secretary? Did she work at anything?

'Come along, then,' said Philip. He bent over his wife and kissed her tenderly. 'Have a good rest, my darling,' he said, 'and when you two have had your little talk, I'll be up again to see you.'

'Thank you, sweetheart,' said Mary. 'Do stop worrying about me. I'm quite comfortable today. Hardly any pain!'

Over lunch, Philip talked about the garden, the neighbours, and his retirement. 'Can't think why I was an actor so long,' he said. 'Didn't want to live on Mary's money, I suppose. Pride . . .' He smiled.

'Has Mary always had money?'

'Yes – though that isn't why I married her.' He sounded defensive now.

106

'I didn't imagine it was,' replied June. 'It never occurred to me. Do you know why Mary wants to see me?'

'I think so. We haven't discussed it because it was her own idea, and she's so set on it that I didn't want to worry her by objecting to it. Anyway, whatever she wants these days I want for her. I can't think what it's going to be like when she's gone. She has always been my saviour. I owe everything to her.'

'Does she know about us?'

'Well of course. She did, right from the start.'

June could hardly believe her ears.

'But you told me she didn't. You even accused *me* of telling her – after South Africa!'

'Did I?'

'You know you did.'

'I don't remember. There have had to be many evasions in my life.'

June stuck grimly to her questioning.

'Doesn't she mind about us?'

'She understands. She has always understood.'

'Do you regret our affair?'

'If it wasn't you it would have been someone else,' he said flatly.

'That's not very polite,' said June. 'After all, I was in love with you for years.'

'Yes,' he said. 'I'm sorry.'

'How do you feel about us now?'

'How do you?' he countered.

'I don't really know,' said June. 'Pretty bewildered, at the moment.'

He seemed to understand and said, 'I suppose so,' vaguely.

'Nothing is like I thought it would be.'

'No, I suppose not.'

June wanted to ask about Mary's illness, but Philip had started his humming again and it was as though the years

107

between them had never been; as though they had met so long ago that they could hardly remember one another. It certainly seemed that all her loving had only created a waste land.

And then she remembered her recurring dream of the flowerless garden and the high fences. Perhaps a part of her had always known how bleak the central ground of her loving had really been?

After lunch she went for a solitary walk in the garden, and wandered down to the lake. A grey squirrel bounced across the grass then shinned up a tree, and there were ducks on the water. When she returned to the house, Philip was nowhere to be seen, so she went upstairs to her room and lay on the bed. She tried to read. She tried to sleep. But rest eluded her.

CHAPTER FIFTEEN

At four forty-five exactly, the nurse came to fetch her to Mary's room.

The fire was lit and a table had been set by the bed, with a silver tea service and two silver muffin dishes containing hot buttered toast and small hot scones. There were sandwiches on two large plates decorated with roses, and there was thick cream and home-made jam.

Once again Mary was sitting up, propped by her pillows. She was flushed from sleep, now, and looked quite attractive. 'Perhaps you'll pour out for me,' she said. 'Philip usually does. Did Cook give you a good meal?'

'Marvellous.'

'I'm glad. Philip has a good appetite, and I don't want her to be careless because I'm not around.'

'She wasn't careless.'

They finished their tea, then Mary pulled her fluffy white bed jacket more closely round her and said, 'I haven't the energy I used to have, unfortunately, so I hope you will forgive me if I come straight to the point. You were in love with my husband for many years, weren't you?'

'Yes,' replied June, uncomfortably.

'Are you in love with him now?' Mary was fiddling with the satin bow on the jacket, and avoiding June's eyes.

'No.'

'Ah, I'm sorry.' June looked at her in surprise. 'You see,

I'm worried about him after I die, and I hoped perhaps you could help?'

'Help? In what way?' June was disturbed at once by the turn the conversation had taken.

'I brought you here to tell you the whole story,' said Mary. 'Do you mind?'

'Of course not.'

'I thought it might help you to help him,' said Mary. 'It's grotesque and unbelievable, but true – and I want you to know it. It can't hurt anyone now.' She pushed a wisp of grey hair away from her eyes, and sighed deeply.

'I met Philip when he was in terrible trouble. We were in the same repertory company together up North, in 1938, and he had become engaged to the very beautiful juvenile in the company. She wasn't a nice girl, but so lovely that you couldn't blame anyone for falling for her, and Philip was deeply in love with her; so deeply that he told her his tragedy. He wanted to marry her, you see, and thought she should know.'

June felt too inadequate to think of anything encouraging to say, so she sat back in the hard little chair, and tried to seem at her ease.

'Unfortunately the girl found the story ludicrous as well as horrifying, and laughed. And Philip went berserk and attacked her ...'

'How awful!' said June.

'Yes,' replied Mary, almost brusquely. 'Luckily she was a strong girl, and managed to get away – but she had the marks on her neck for quite a while ...'

June was deeply shocked. 'D'you mean – you think he might have killed her?' she asked, horrified.

'He himself was afraid so,' answered Mary. 'And in view of his history, I'm not surprised.'

'His history?'

Mary pressed a trembling hand to her mouth.

'Fortunately for Philip, the girl was unpopular with all the women because she was after the men all the time, so the general feeling was that she had brought the trouble on herself. She left the company, swearing that Philip had tried to murder her – but, thank heaven, she didn't go to the police.'

'My God!' murmured June. 'How terrible!'

'Yes, terrible,' agreed Mary. 'Afterwards he was devastated by what he had done, and very nearly had a breakdown. Luckily for us both, I was in love with him, and I managed to get him to trust me enough to tell me the whole story, and when he trusted me, he asked me to marry him, and we have been very happy ever since.'

June stared at her in amazement, but she continued calmly, 'I don't know how much he has told you about his family, although I know he hasn't told you the truth about his father.'

She fell silent for a while, and June waited uncomfortably; Mary continued, with an effort.

'Philip comes from a farming family in Yorkshire, you know – a bleak grey farmhouse, in bleak lonely countryside. His maternal grandfather owned the farm, but they made a poor living. From the first, Philip's father disliked farming, and when Philip was very small he managed to escape by getting a job as a commercial traveller. He had done well at school, and was a bright young man as well as extremely good looking, so he made a little money and for a time was happy, but then the old grandfather died, and he was needed back on the farm, and that was the beginning of the trouble.

'Philip was seven and his brother was nine when their father came back for good. Philip was overjoyed, because his father was his hero. While he was a traveller he had often come home laden with gifts for the children, and Philip had kept every one of his. He was also his father's favourite, which meant a great deal to him. Perhaps more than it should.

111

'Philip's mother was a dark-haired, handsome woman with a wicked temper and flashing black eyes. She was powerfully built; taller than her husband, and she was a scold. Philip's father, like Philip, was a small man; he was no weakling, but he was gentle-mannered and peace-loving, and this seemed to arouse his wife's unsleeping anger. She openly despised him for not being even as good a farmer as her father, and endlessly nagged him for being what she called "soft-foolish". The rows between the two of them were constant and things went from bad to worse, until one night, after they had been entertaining relatives to high tea, and she had humiliated him beyond his bearing in front of them, he went for her with a hammer ... and killed her.'

'How terrible!' repeated June. 'Poor little man ...'

'The farm was sold, and the children went to an uncle and aunt whom Philip hated. They were stern and chapel-going, and the boys were never allowed to forget their "disgrace" – not that this would have been possible for Philip anyway, with his temperament. What's more, when the time came for his father to be hanged, Philip was taken to see him in prison to say goodbye. Imagine that! He was only ten.'

Mary had small beads of sweat round her lips, and she dabbed at them angrily with a handkerchief.

'So you can see why that cruel girl in the repertory company so affected him. She was tall and dominating, like his mother ... And you can also see why we never had children ...' Mary shut her eyes. 'It was a great sorrow for me not having children, but with Philip the son of a murderer, of course it was out of the question.'

June remembered Philip once telling her that Mary wanted children, and felt deeply sorry for her. Then she remembered Philip's violent attack on her in the dressing room, and wondered with a shiver how close she herself had been to death. She asked slowly, 'Has Philip still a violent temper?'

112

'He has never lost his temper with me during the whole course of our marriage,' said Mary.

'And you were never frightened that one day he might do so?'

Mary looked at her coldly. 'No, I wasn't,' she said. 'We understand each other too well.'

'What happened to Philip's brother?'

'Philip's brother was much tougher and less imaginative than Philip. He was also much loved by both the uncle and the aunt; indeed, he still lives near them with his wife and three children.'

'Oh, so he had children?'

'He married his childhood sweetheart, and she's a stolid sort of person. So is he, if it comes to that. But Philip early found that he was the possessor of a powerful sexual drive which he found hard to control. His nightmare was that he might follow in his father's footsteps, because the girls he usually found attractive were tall and dark and domineering. Of course he was terribly mixed up emotionally; so mixed up that he was still a virgin by the time of his engagement, and indeed by the time he married me!' She looked defiantly at June.

'He was never romantically in love with me, but strangely, I believe that I helped him, especially as I was in love with him, and he knew he could trust me. During the war he was in the Pioneer Corps, because he had flat feet. He was very ashamed of this, but I told him that he was every bit as essential as anyone in a more glamorous regiment. I was still an actress, and managed to get a job in ENSA in a comedy called *Lady from Edinburgh*. We met up in Lille when I went overseas. He was faithful to me then, I'm sure, and I loved him for it. I am still in love with him, and not many women who have been married for as long as I have would be able to say that, would they?' She smiled proudly.

'It was of course inevitable that he would in time be

113

unfaithful to me, but I realised that it was of the utmost importance to him that he should be able to find himself sexually, and learn from his own experience to dissociate sex from the nightmare of his father. You see, I forgot to tell you that Philip's father was sexually obsessed with his wife all through their marriage, and that Philip's uncle and aunt had blamed the murder on this. "A disgusting and wicked love," they had called it. "Shocking, and it led to madness and death." "God pays," his aunt used to say. "Oh, yes, God pays." And she'd look triumphant. She frightened Philip.

'In a way I encouraged Philip's affairs, but I always made him tell me about them, so that if he turned to violence he would be involving me as a sort of accessory. It was quite a strain, but he was grateful to me for understanding his needs, and we had that most rewarding of all relationships, a profoundly loving friendship between a man and a woman. Then you came into his life . . . and he felt more deeply about you than the others . . . Oh, yes, he did, whatever you may think . . . and of course he told me all about you.'

She stopped talking and breathed deeply, then she said, 'I didn't approve of you, a clergyman's daughter, for behaving as you did with a married man – and you were also so surprisingly unlike the girls he usually liked – but Philip was in love with you physically and there was little either of us could do about it. He had to prove to himself that he could actually make passionate love to a woman, without violence, but he was determined not to let you break up our marriage, which he knew was the most important relationship in his life. You didn't care, did you, that he was happily married? All you cared about was the sex.'

June saw the hatred in Mary's eyes.

'Sometimes he found it pretty hard going loving the two of us, and with you always after him, and many times I was frightened that I might lose him to you, and I didn't know what might happen to him then. But it was all right in the end

114

because finally the "shooting incident", as we always call it, brought him to his senses, and he ceased to care for you. For one thing it brought him notoriety – something he dreaded. For another it was a reminder of violence.'

Mary closed her eyes for a moment, and leaned back against the pillows. June sat motionless, wondering how much strength was left in her frail body. Darkness had fallen while Mary was speaking.

'Mary,' she said gently, 'is there something I can get you? ... A glass of water? ... Shall I turn on the light, perhaps?'

Mary roused herself. 'Yes, do. No water, thank you ... I feel a little tired now, but there's something else I must say. Would you be kind enough to draw the curtains? And perhaps you could make up the fire a little?'

June rose stiffly and did as she was asked. Why am I here? she thought unhappily, listening to the intimate secrets of a man I should never have loved, from a woman who is dying? She returned to Mary's bedside with a feeling of over-whelming reluctance.

'June, dear,' went on Mary urgently, 'I have a request to make. It's the real reason why I asked you to come. When I'm gone, will you keep an eye on Philip for me? He has been through so much, and I believe we all of us only have so much capacity for hardship.'

June gazed at her.

'You have done us both much harm, and yet I had hoped that, since he was your first love, he might still be important to you ...' The sweat was standing out on Mary's forehead, and she dipped a handkerchief in water then dampened her brow.

'How on earth can *I* keep an eye on him?' exclaimed June in alarm. 'I told you – I no longer love him. Besides, my husband has never forgiven me for being unfaithful to him, and he is very angry that I have come to you now. I can't possibly take on the responsibility of Philip, you must

115

understand that. I only came because I felt I owed you something.'

'Quite right. And Philip too.'

'What do I owe Philip?' demanded June. 'He seduced me when I was eighteen!'

'He says you threw yourself at him – and yet he gave you a long-lasting love, a first love,' retorted Mary. 'Surely you owe him something for that!' She dipped the handkerchief again, wrung it out, and wiped her face wearily over and over again.

'If his brother managed to get over the murder, couldn't Philip have done the same?' asked June.

'For heaven's sake!' Mary was angry. 'Haven't you understood what I've been telling you? Can't you see what Philip has suffered? Don't you know how fortunate you are that, after you had forced him into a sexual relationship, he had the courage and the control to live normally with you – to have an affair with you that didn't come seriously to grief?'

'*Seriously to grief!*' June thought wryly. Certainly at times it had come seriously to grief for her! And she *hadn't* thrown herself at Philip – not at the beginning, anyway; but she couldn't say that here. She said aloud, hating herself for saying it when Mary was so distraught but needing to justify herself, 'It made me very unhappy.'

'And Philip too. You were unhappy because he was a married man and rejected you, that's all. For no other reason. Philip was unhappy for many deeper reasons. And so was I. You know, I find it astonishing that you don't seem to understand the importance of what I've been telling you about Philip. You professed to love him for two decades and you didn't know the first thing about him.'

'How could I? He never told me any of this . . .'

Mary overrode her with growing excitement. 'His whole life was warped by his father's terrible crime. He has suffered terribly. Now I am dying, and he may need you, and yet you feel no sense of responsibility!'

116

'Philip won't need me,' said June flatly. 'He has never ever needed me except physically.'

Mary became calmer and said more quietly, 'We've all suffered, I see that now. Extra-marital affairs very often make people suffer. And an unrequited love, I suppose, brings great unhappiness; it becomes an obsession – and obsession is terrible to live with. But think of the horror of Philip's obsession! Yours was as nothing compared to his. And you wouldn't leave him alone, Philip said, no matter how often he told you to, so if you were unhappy you brought it on yourself. I did neither of you harm, but you harmed me. And Philip didn't set out to harm either of us. His physical need was strong and the circumstances were very special.' She looked at June pleadingly. She was breathing hard and her small thin hands clutched at the sheets. 'He *will* need your help, I'm sure. Please think about it,' she said. 'It is very important to me. And you've been married all along, so that's no excuse.'

She twisted her head restlessly on the pillows, and silence fell.

It was true. Everything that Mary had said was true. June's great love was just 'an extra-marital affair' which had done nothing but harm; and her obsession, the core of her being, had been, as Mary had said, as nothing as compared with Philip's. The very centre of her living had been founded on a sin, and she suddenly thought of herself with great distaste. Philip had been right to call her a whore – she was indeed a scarlet woman, although in her own eyes she had only loved him with all her heart. Nowadays everyone had affairs with everyone as a matter of course, and it was hardly something to make such a fuss about – yet anything to do with Philip she had always magnified a hundred times. Anyway, it was over now – and this time for good. The magic – the splendour, the fulfilment and the pain – over.

117

'I wish I had known about Philip sooner,' she said at last. 'It was unfair of him to keep me in the dark.'

'It was unfair of you to try to take Philip from me,' retorted Mary. 'He is my husband.'

'You're right,' said June. 'I've behaved very badly. You're a remarkable woman, Mary, and Philip is a very lucky man.'

'Thank you,' answered Mary simply. 'I'm not going to plead with you because I'm too tired, although that's what I feel like doing. Philip needs help, and I'd be grateful if you'd look after him. Forgive me, this conversation is taking it out of me.' She sighed deeply. 'I can only repeat, think about it,' she said. 'Promise me you'll think about it.'

'I'll think about it,' said June. That at least she could promise: it would be surprising if she didn't think about it for many years to come! Mary began crying, the tears pouring down her face. 'Please, please don't cry!' said June. 'I can't bear it.'

'It's weakness,' said Mary feebly. 'I don't usually cry. Thank you for caring. Philip told me you were a nice girl.'

June nearly called out at this, but managed to control herself. Mary found a second tiny lace-edged handkerchief from under her pillow, and blew her nose on it, then shut her eyes again, lying once more against the pillows, white and drained.

'Are you sure I can't get you something?' asked June, alarmed at her pallor. 'A pain killer of some sort? A drink? Shall I call Philip, or the nurse?'

'No. Nothing,' said Mary. 'I'll be all right soon. Dear June, thank you for coming. It was kind of you.' She smiled slightly, and added, 'And thank you for failing to take Philip from me. Perhaps one day you'll be glad to know that through you, and because of you, he was able to have a sexual relationship with someone he cared about, so you did great good as well as harm.

'I won't see you tomorrow,' she went on. 'I think we've said

118

all we have to say. We're not really the same kind of people at all, are we? Stay the night as we have arranged, and cheer Philip up at dinner. He has little enough to amuse him now.'

'I will,' said June, although it was the last thing on earth she wanted to do. 'I'll do my best.'

Mary rang the bell beside her. 'I'm ringing for Nurse,' she said. 'I ought to take my medicine. We dine at eight, but there will be drinks in the drawing room at six, and it is ten minutes to, now. Philip will be anxious to know if our talk went well, so tell him it did, won't you?'

'Of course.'

'Goodbye, June. Take care of yourself.'

'Goodbye, Mary. I wish you weren't so ill. Have you much pain?'

'No. No. They keep it under control, and I shall be gone in a few months. Not long to bear it.'

June leaned forward to kiss her, but fractionally Mary drew herself away, murmuring 'Thank you.' Then she shut her eyes tight like a child, and lay still and rigid.

June left her, closing the door gently behind her, and went down the stairs to Philip in the drawing room.

She didn't enjoy the rest of her stay, but she did her best, as Mary had asked her to, to entertain Philip at dinner. He seemed in better spirits. Nearly all his conversation was about Mary, but occasionally he asked about friends and colleagues in the theatre. He asked very little about Bruce, and hardly talked about their past together at all.

At last June told him that she knew about his father, and he said, 'Oh, yes?', which wasn't encouraging.

'And about you, and the girl in the repertory company.'

'Ah,' said Philip.

'Why didn't you tell me about it?' demanded June. 'It would have made things so much easier.'

'Perhaps it would,' he said vaguely. 'I don't know. Living

119

with that fearsome aunt and uncle taught me to hide nearly all my feelings. They loved my brother, but I couldn't get on with either of them. Everything I did seemed to be wrong for them, so I learned to be secretive about anything that mattered to me.'

'But I was in love with you.'

'Yes.'

Suddenly June felt sorry for him again and she said impulsively, 'I'm so sorry, Philip! You must have had an appallingly difficult time!'

'Yes.'

'And I made things no easier!'

'No.' Then he said expressionlessly, 'One can get so easily lost in the twin catacombs of love and sex.'

June looked at him sharply. 'What an odd thing to say!' she exclaimed. He didn't answer.

There was a long silence, then she asked awkwardly, 'What will you do when Mary dies?' and he replied, 'Live here, I suppose. What else?' in a toneless voice.

She asked him if he liked Suffolk.

'Of course I do,' he said, 'it's Mary's birthplace.'

This seemed excessive, but June struggled on. 'Do you remember our affair with any pleasure at all, darling? I feel terrible that I did so much harm. I didn't mean to.'

'Well, we had a good time,' replied Philip absently, as though he were being polite to some colleague from the past.

At last she said, 'Have you any love left for me now, Philip?'

'Of course, my dear. Haven't you?'

'Yes,' she said, 'of course.' And since she was lying, she thought he might be lying, too. It was all inexpressibly depressing.

She went to bed at ten o'clock, to the four-poster so like her own at home, staring up at the darkness and going over what Mary had told her over and over again. Philip's father a

120

murderer. Murderer. Murderer. Murderer. The words echoed and re-echoed in her brain. The sins of the father had nearly ruined Philip's life and Mary's telling of it had reduced June's love to a nonsense, and her self-respect to rubble. And Mary had looked so exhausted when she finished talking that June was worried for her.

When she slept she dreamed of a flowerless garden with high fences, inhabited by a shabby solitary man, whom she recognised with fear as Philip's father.

CHAPTER SIXTEEN

She didn't see Mary again, but Philip came to the front door the next morning to see her off. He was looking quite smart and several times he smiled that charming smile which took so many years off his age, and which long ago had so often melted her heart. He seemed in strangely good spirits and kissed her warmly on the cheek as she got into the car. As she went down the drive she looked back – and he was standing looking after her, waving vigorously. She turned a corner, and put her foot down hard on the accelerator.

The weather was still beautiful, but she was in no mood for scenery. She was dead tired after her almost sleepless night, and still enormously depressed. What she had felt for Philip had always seemed so important. Now the kaleidoscope had shifted. Philip no less than Mary was a stranger to her, and all she wanted to do now was to put things straight with her family. It wouldn't be easy. Things had been a long time going wrong. What's more, she didn't look forward to telling Bruce that she had more or less promised to keep an eye on Philip after Mary died.

She wondered if Bruce had read her letter. Surely he would understand? With this visit behind her, perhaps they could at least talk again? He still hadn't left home. Perhaps he didn't really want to? Perhaps they could get together again after all?

Pippa's wedding was still ahead of them, and it would need a lot of organisation (not to mention money) so they'd have to work in harness for a bit. They both liked Charles, and they'd have to meet his parents and behave like parents themselves – which should bring them closer together. But would it?

Pippa would need her help as well as Bruce's – more than Bruce's in many ways. June was still angry about Pippa's behaviour at the party, but who was she to talk? She'd made a fistful of mistakes herself, and over a far longer period of time. Besides, the child was starting out on a new life – and June certainly wished her well. It would be good for her to have someone of her own age for once, to love and cherish: her infatuation for Bruce would have to take second place. And perhaps, without Pippa acting as a barrier between them, she and Bruce would get on better.

But there was still Mandy.

What was Bruce going to do about her? Her youthful adoration flattered him and flattery was sweet, even necessary to him, after the humiliations of her own unrelenting obsession with Philip.

If Bruce left her she would only have herself to blame. She wanted him to be happy – but was Mandy the right wife for him? Surely not!

Bruce. The linchpin of her life. How wonderful it would be if they could start again, if he could forgive her, understand the muddle she'd been in, and trust her enough to believe that she'd never get into such a stupid muddle again!

At any rate there was no competition from her secret life any more. She was at Bruce's disposal from now on, if he'd have her, and at Pippa's too. She was lucky enough to have her career to fall back on if everything else failed, but she mustn't let it. A career to fall back on – that showed how spoilt she was. So many actors and actresses, desperately under-employed, ambitious, and willing to make their career the most important thing in their lives, and here she was treating hers as second best!

She looked at her watch. She should be home in time for a

pre-lunch drink. Thank goodness – she needed it! She glanced into the car mirror. Yes, she was looking OK, in spite of her restless night. The dress was one Bruce liked, and her hair was looking its best. She was in her forties, but if you didn't know it, you might not guess. She'd be home in three-quarters of an hour. Only three-quarters of an hour! Pray heaven they'd both be there! Perhaps the past could be relegated to the past at last, and the future, the wonderful future, would be different.

When she reached home there was no one in, and two letters were waiting for her on the hall table. One was in Bruce's handwriting, and one in Pippa's. She left her overnight case in the hall, and went straight into the drawing room. She threw herself on the sofa with a dry mouth, and opened Bruce's letter first.

Dear June,

I've left home. I'm sure you'll understand why. It was only a matter of time anyway, wasn't it? Mandy and I have decided to marry as soon as we can, so I'll be asking for a divorce directly after Pippa's wedding. I'm sure you'll be agreeable. We'll sort out money, possessions and all those dreary details whenever you like. You won't find me unreasonable. We'll have to get in touch about Pippa's wedding very soon as she still wants that whopping white one, so I'll ring you tomorrow.

I hope you had a good weekend, and that Mary's state of health wasn't too upsetting, poor woman! I hope too that you found lover-boy all that you hoped.

Bruce

There was not one word about her letter. Her gamble had failed!

June began crying, and poured herself a vodka and tonic.

124

Her hands were shaking. It served her right, and it was inevitable. It had been stupid of her to hope.

It was some time before she opened Pippa's letter.

Pippa's handwriting was very large, and though apparently beautifully formed, very illegible.

Mother darling,

I have thought about this for the past couple of weeks as of course I didn't want to hurt you, but I have gone to live at a friend's flat in Clapham. You know her, and she's very nice. It's Alice Ledbetter. Daddy has just told me that he's leaving too, so it may seem rather a cruel time to go, but you're so wonderfully self-reliant and disciplined that I'm sure you won't miss me too much. I know I upset you by springing my engagement to Charles so suddenly on you at the party, and as I shall be seeing him a great deal in the next few weeks it's probably better if we don't keep on meeting under your roof, so to speak. Of course you and I will be seeing lots of each other, which will be lovely, as there'll be such lots to see to about the wedding, and what with that and the play, you won't have time to feel too lonely.

I'm sorry, darling, to spring this suddenly on you too, but I know you'll understand.

I'll ring you tomorrow morning. Have a good show tonight, and I hope you enjoyed the weekend.

Lots and lots of love, darling,

Your Pippa.

Now June was shaking with anger. Little bitch! she thought. Little bitch! She knows quite well how much she's hurting me, and she knows I can't do a thing about it!

She shivered suddenly and got up to light the fire. She then went to the kitchen and made herself a sandwich which

125

she took back on a tray to the drawing room. The telephone bell rang and she picked up the receiver.

It was Philip.

'You left some gloves behind. I thought you might miss them and wonder where they were. Shall I send them to you? They look quite new.'

'No. Don't bother. I hardly ever wear gloves.'

'Well we don't need them,' said Philip. 'I'll send them anyway.'

'OK. Thanks. And thank you for the weekend. I enjoyed it very much, although I hated seeing Mary so ill.'

'You've done her a lot of good. It was kind of you to come. She asked me to send you her best wishes. Goodbye, June. Take care of yourself.'

'Goodbye, Philip. My love to Mary.'

She rang off and the silence in the house became an intrusion.

From now on, she was on her own.

PART THREE

Afterwards

CHAPTER SEVENTEEN

My obsession had gone, but so, too, had my family!

Years earlier, I had consulted a psychiatrist during one of my bouts of depression. I had told him about my wretched condition and his reply had shocked me.

'My advice to you is to abandon hope.'

'But I can't!' I objected. 'How can I?'

'If you don't,' he replied, 'you simply prolong the status quo. Philip is not in love with you. You are in love with him. Because he's not in love with you, he'll never change. You are the only person who can change the pattern. If you want relief, that's the only way to get it.'

Of course I never abandoned hope – then, or for years after. Our obsessions are precious to us. Now, however, without my volition, hope had become irrelevant, because the obsession had vanished in a puff of smoke.

I was desperately sorry for both Philip and Mary, and I cursed the arid years of my serfdom – but I was free at last, I told myself, and could return to reality. I would get nowhere with self-pity! There was the rest of my life to live. I was in good health, I had money, a home, a job and many friends. I must salvage what I could, and thank my lucky stars for my blessings.

At first, listening to Mary, I had felt a contemptible fool. Now, as I struggled to resurrect a life of my own, I came to feel that it was not necessary to take the whole guilt upon myself. I had done my best to cope with a destructive love affair, and if I had failed, then Philip was as much to blame as I. I could understand his conduct now, but that did not mean I could justify it: he was much older than I and had been in a position of trust as my tutor at drama school when the affair began and had known how inexperienced I was. He had been both selfish and callous.

My two worst times during that first year alone were Pippa's wedding, and the first visit to my lawyer about my divorce.

The wedding was to be a magnificent affair at St George's, Hanover Square with a reception afterwards at the Royal Garden Hotel. Two hundred guests had been invited, and the wedding presents filled the dining room to overflowing. Pippa came almost daily to sort them out and write lists and thank-you letters. She was in high spirits these days and made a great fuss of me, and a great parade of deferring to my wishes. She had asked my advice about her wedding dress, and she also consulted me about clothes for the bridesmaids and the four little pages. She tried to get me to help find a house for her and Charles, too, but this I refused to do: I knew that she would, quite rightly, have entirely different views from mine about where and how she should live, so it seemed a waste of time.

The fact that Bruce had left me so precipitately was not only an agonising emotional wrench for me, but excruciatingly embarrassing, and the wedding and reception only magnified the problem. I was having to see a large number of people who had no idea how to deal with the situation, so never mentioned Bruce's name – as though I had become suddenly but shamefully widowed, which in a way I suppose I had. (See this as funny, I told myself savagely.) I had been forced to see Bruce from time to time, which became progressively harder for me. He never once enquired about my visit to Philip, and his manner towards me was always coldly polite. Once or twice I started to ask him about my letter, but I never managed to finish the sentence. When the time came to give Pippa away, he looked heart-stoppingly handsome and very proud of her. The wedding was a splendid occasion and I seemed to be the only one not enjoying myself.

Our uncontested divorce went through in due course, and Bruce married Mandy. As he had promised there were no arguments. He left me the house and most of the furniture and pictures, and he was generous about money; but he seemed to have no wish to be friendly or to see me. He and Mandy found a large flat near Regent's Park, and I never saw Mandy at all.

I swear I tried to deal with my life as best as I could, but I found many unexpected difficulties. As a successful actress I had always had plenty of independence and a life remarkably free from domesticity. This didn't alter. I continued to be treated (as all actresses are treated) as an equal to men in my job, and as someone rather special, socially, so I had a great deal going for me. What I had not bargained for was the reaction of my female social acquaintances, many of whom I had regarded as friends, if not particularly close friends. A number of them dropped me at once now that I was on my own, perhaps fearing me as a threat to their husbands as I still hadn't lost all attraction; or perhaps they were simply bored by a woman without a man in tow. Luckily the attitude of my actress friends hardly changed; many in fact had been through marital upheavals themselves and were more forthcoming than they had been, and one or two were blessedly sympathetic. Because Bruce and I were both in the theatre we had been together a great deal at work and at play. This meant that I had no 'special' woman friend, since Bruce had filled the rôle of confidant (except about Philip), and he was not too keen on dealing with more than one woman at a time!

The attitude of most of the men I knew also changed

radically. The ones who were attracted seemed to think that, now I was free of Bruce, I was available as an easy lay. This shouldn't really have shocked me, but it did. I realised now that Bruce had protected me in a number of unsuspected ways. As his wife I had been treated with a certain deference. I had of course been propositioned from time to time, but not made to think of myself as merchandise. What was equally undignified, and even less palatable, was that the men who preferred younger women made me feel like a pane of glass: they looked through me to a more interesting vista beyond, and any kind of conversation with me, however trivial, seemed to demand manners and an effort too great for them to make. This was especially true of men in their late forties and early fifties, who often need girls half their age to boost their dwindling vanity.

I still went out a good deal but, even when I was out, I felt lonely for Bruce, and many of the places I went to, and the people that I saw, reminded me too much of him. I was always on the look out for him, but seldom saw him. I couldn't make up my mind whether I wanted to see him or not.

I had lost him, and didn't want to be reminded of my loss, but he'd been a marvellous friend, and I hated losing that friendship. It was probably another area where I should 'abandon hope'!

I could see where I had gone wrong about him – indeed I would have been feeble-minded if I couldn't! But now I tried to explore why I had so signally failed with Pippa.

I saw very little of her now. After their Caribbean honeymoon, she and Charles had moved in to a flat in Knightsbridge. I was asked to tea occasionally, and even more rarely to lunch, but I seldom spoke intimately to Pippa because I hardly saw her on her own. All the same, I pursued a small but relentless enquiry with all the mothers of daughters I knew, to find out how they had fared – and quite soon a strange pattern appeared which proved my case not to be unusual, but no less lamentable for that.

A great many mothers found daughters difficult, although it was true that a few had far better relationships with their daughters than their sons. The successful ones I left alone for the time being, as being irrelevant to my enquiry; but among the others I discovered that, in by far the greatest proportion of cases, the daughters were father-orientated to a marked degree. But it was when I spoke to mothers with only children, and those children daughters, that I found a real parallel with my case – especially if the mothers were pretty, as I had been. No less than six times among these people, the daughters had been the cause of the divorce.

In three cases the daughters had threatened to marry entirely unsuitable men, because they were 'unhappy at home because Mummy doesn't love me'. Yet when the parents had split, the daughters returned to the *mothers*, having broken off with the boyfriends. (Apparently all were upset that the husbands had now married again!) One daughter had become a nun but had returned to the outside world just before taking her final vows, directly after her parents were divorced; another had had a fashionable wedding which only lasted until the father's remarriage, and another again had had a breakdown until the parents' divorce.

Naturally I had no specialist understanding of the individual problems which may have led to these developments, but it did seem to mean that, badly as I must have mismanaged my own situation, a great many other people had mismanaged badly, too.

This was a comfort. It shouldn't have been, but when one is unhappy it is a help to know that one is not alone. Like me, many women had alienated their daughters. Like me, many women had husbands who had left them for someone younger, and many again had had unhappy love affairs. I

133

was as ordinary as it was possible to be, and all the guilt in the world wasn't going to undo the mistakes I had made; besides, I was far luckier than most of the others. I had a career which I loved.

I thought back constantly over the times we had had together, Pippa and I, and in all the memory pictures I had of her, she was turning adoringly to Bruce, and he to her. I hadn't loved her enough to straighten out her neuroses. That was the nub of it.

I remembered a time in Greece, on holiday, when Bruce and I were so happy together (even after the shooting incident) that she must have noticed how extra close we were and decided to put a stop to it. It was one o'clock in the morning. Bruce and I were in our hotel bedroom getting ready for bed. We were both naked, and Bruce had taken me in his arms when I heard a stifled sob and turned to find Pippa, also naked, weeping silently and rubbing her eyes fiercely with her fists. Bruce put her to bed in her own little room next door and had to spend a long time trying to get her to sleep. When he came back, desire for me had gone, and we were never quite so unselfconscious again when we made love during that holiday.

I remember another time, when I found one of the drawers in my dressing-table half open, and some of my letters from Bruce had vanished. I went straight to Pippa's room where, scarlet-faced with anger, she was burning them in her grate. When I remonstrated with her she spat out words, 'Filthy! How could you and Daddy be so *filthy*?' And nothing I could say to her calmed her, although some days later she seemed to forget the incident, and to behave normally again. I remembered the psychosomatic hysterical illnesses she had when Bruce was too busy to pay her enough attention when I was in a play he had written for me; I remembered the radiance of her smile every time he returned from a trip abroad. I remembered her sulks and tantrums if I crossed her, and her immediate docility if Bruce told her to do what I had said. And above all, I remembered her beauty. Her face at all her ages kept flashing into my mind, and into my dreams. Beautiful. Hostile to me. Closed.

Her relationship with Charles was curious, but seemed to give them both great satisfaction. Charles was besotted by her looks, and head over heels in love with her, and she was kind, loving and protective, and in full command.

The interior of their charming flat behind Harrods was very much her creation, although a great deal of the furniture came from his parents' home in Yorkshire, and very beautiful it was too. As an assistant to an antiques dealer she had learned a lot, and her sense of colour was spectacular. The dining room and hall were vividly bright, the drawing room and bedrooms decorated in gentle smoke colours. She had few pictures as yet, but was already starting to be very knowledgeable, and she had begun to collect china. Collecting, I realised, would interest her. She was totally absorbed in her home, and as usual, fanatically tidy. Charles raved about her cooking, which surprised me, as she had shown no inclination towards it with us; but I was delighted, and her happiness suited her.

They saw a good deal of Bruce and Mandy, Pippa told me, adding that Mandy was very much their own age, which made things easier ('Sorry, Mummy'), and that Bruce was very happy, too. She thought it quite sensible that Bruce and I hardly met. Not easy for Mandy, she said. I had nothing against Mandy, except that I would rather have been Bruce's wife myself, and it seemed sad that more than twenty years of our knowing each other should have to be expunged so totally! However, there it was.

Once I asked Pippa if she wanted children, and she answered coldly that at the moment they were happy as they were. She didn't want to burden Charles with too much responsibility as yet, she said. I invited them both several times to have dinner with me, or lunch over the weekend, but mostly

Pippa refused. They were busy, she said, and Charles wasn't really 'into theatre and actors', which, since Bruce and Mandy also worked in the theatre, surprised me somewhat. When they did come to see me, she always seemed restless, but Charles and I got on well, and I liked him more and more.

Then Mary died. There was a short obituary both in the *Telegraph* and *The Times*. She was the daughter of the (late) third Lord Manningtree, and therefore an 'Honourable' (Philip would have enjoyed that). Her brother now held the title, and there were three sisters and another brother still living. She had been on the board of several charities, and was the founder of an organisation for the support of abused children (which was presumably why she had had a secretary). She was in her mid-sixties, and in the *Telegraph* she was described as actor Philip Goodson's 'adored wife'.

I telephoned him, because it seemed more personal than writing, and was told he was staying with his sister-in-law Lady Beverley for an indefinite period. I then sent him a letter but received no answer.

Three weeks later, on his return home from Lady Beverley's, he shot himself.

I was devastated. I had been no sort of help to him, but even had I tried harder, I don't think it would have made any difference. Mary had been his life-line, as he always said, and he couldn't linger on without her. He had loved her profoundly on a level I had never even guessed at.

Although his going left me numb, it had surprisingly little other effect on me. I had imagined that he would leave an irreplaceable void, but his siren lure had been to my subconscious, and when he went, the lure disappeared even more completely than the vanishing of the obsession which had preceded his death. If I thought about him at all, I was wistfully sad. No more.

To my amazement, Pippa was extremely sympathetic. She

136

telephoned me daily for several weeks, and asked me over whenever she could. She was warm and comforting, and at last we became closer.

I told her a good deal about Philip, and she seemed to understand. She was horrified for him about his father. I didn't tell her that I had only found out about this on my last visit to them, as frankly I was too ashamed, and she wrongly believed that part of the reason I had allowed him in my life for so long was because of it, and gave me credit for it, which made me feel even guiltier. The fact that I had been obsessed interested her so much that I made the mistake of suggesting that she had had a similar obsession for her father. She not only vehemently denied this, but became angry with me for suggesting it. I nearly lost her friendship.

I didn't know why she was so interested in Philip, and couldn't understand how she could be so tolerant about our affair at last, but was only thankful that that was how she felt. I asked her why, of course, and she murmured that it explained so many things, and when I asked her what things, she said, 'You didn't really concentrate on Daddy, and it made him miserable so I tried to make up for it.'

'Is that true?' I asked in astonishment. 'It seemed to me that you always loved your father much much more than you loved me.'

'Did I?' she asked. 'Well, perhaps I did. I adored him, and he adored me, but I do really think it was because I thought he was lonely. I remember once you shot a man, and I think I was always frightened one day you might shoot me.'

I was appalled.

'Shot a man?' I exclaimed in horror. 'What the hell are you talking about?'

'Well, shot *at* him, then. You *tried* to shoot him, though – Nanette said – and from then on I was scared of you.'

'What absolute rubbish!' I replied angrily. 'I never shot or tried to shoot anyone. The man was Philip. He'd been to

137

dinner with me, and had been playing up a girl in his company. *She* got jealous and took a shot at him when he left the house. It wasn't me.'

'Nanette said it was you. She said you'd do it to me if I was a naughty girl, and she said that you were lucky not to go to prison.'

'I don't believe it!' I now felt impatient as well as angry. 'You were only six at the time and you're twenty-two now. Do you really mean to tell me that you've thought your mother was a failed murderess for sixteen years, and you've never once brought up the subject until now?'

Pippa flushed. 'Well, it's what Nanette told me,' she mumbled, 'and she said if I did ever bring up the subject with you, I'd be in danger.'

'Oh come on!' I retorted. 'This is getting ridiculous – the girl who shot at Philip was given an eighteen-month prison sentence. And what about your father? Did you talk to him about his "murderous" wife?'

'No.'

'Why not, if I scared you so? If I was a danger to you?'

'I didn't think he'd believe me. He loved you so much.'

'He loved you so much too, Pippa. D'you think he'd have allowed you to stay in the house with me if I was a danger to you? Tell me the truth, now. Do you really believe I shot at a man? Whatever Nanette told you?'

'I think in a way I never believed it,' said Pippa slowly. 'But I wanted to believe it. It was exciting, and a secret, and it was fun being frightened; like living in a fairy tale with ogres and giants, and I loved fairy tales. Nanette was very jealous of you, you know. She thought it was unfair that you had two men in love with you – Daddy and Philip – when she had none. She wasn't physically attractive and she resented it. She got hysterical, too, and told whopping lies. Quite a rum person to be in charge of a child, but she loved me, and we were very close.'

138

'And you remember all this from when you were six?'

'Yes,' said Pippa, seriously. 'In a way I do.'

'Why did you never tell me about it?'

'You were so remote,' said Pippa. 'You epitomised glamour and wickedness and fame and beauty, and you went around in a cloud of scent. I too was jealous of you.'

I felt slightly sick. 'And are you now?' I asked carefully.

'Oh yes. It's a habit and it will never go.'

'There's nothing to be jealous of, now.'

'It's a habit,' she repeated, and then, 'I do remember it all, you know. Funny.'

'What?'

'All this shooting that seemed to go on around Philip.'

'Hardly "all this shooting",' I said. I found that I disliked her saying this.

'Two lots is already more than happens to most people.'

'Perhaps that silly girl's shooting all those years ago gave him the idea,' I said.

'Perhaps.' She smiled. 'Well, I'm glad you've talked to me about him at last. He was always such a part of my life.'

Again I was astounded. 'Was he? I was only with him once again after that time, and that was only because your father advised me to take the job.'

'He was part of my nightmares,' said Pippa gravely. 'I thought he would come and take you away one day and that Daddy and I would have to fend for ourselves.'

'Surely you'd have liked that,' I smiled. 'Then you could have had Daddy all to yourself!'

'I might not have been allowed to stay with Daddy,' said Pippa. 'I might have had to live with you, without him.'

'Ah,' I said. 'I see what you mean!'

She laughed. 'I didn't mean it like that!' she said. 'You know what I mean.'

'Yes,' I said. 'I know what you mean.'

I was still angry, and disappointed that we were on

139

opposite sides of the fence once again. It had been good being friends with Pippa. She was fun to be with when she wanted to be, and lately had seemed to have a far warmer personality than I had thought. I wondered, though, about her interest in obsessions – but, true to myself, stupidly never probed. Diffidence can be a sin.

CHAPTER EIGHTEEN

After a while I decided to sell the house in Chelsea. We were well into the depressed eighties. The swinging sixties seemed an age ago. House prices had spiralled, everyone seemed hard up, and I felt a little ostentatious living so grandly on my own. I rang Bruce to tell him what I was doing, and to offer to share the sale price with him.

He sounded surprisingly pleased to hear me, and seemed touched at my offer. 'Wouldn't hear of it,' he said, 'but I do appreciate the thought, I really do. How are you? I often think about you and wonder.'

'Do you?' I asked, trying to keep my voice under control. 'Me, too.'

'Are you well? Happy? I know you're working hard, and I'm delighted.'

'Yes, indeed. Thank God for work, and yes, I'm well and happy.'

'That's good. I was worried about Philip's suicide and how it might affect you. Sad, poor chap.'

'Yes. He just couldn't survive Mary's death.'

'So it seemed.' He sounded cautious.

'It's all a long and involved tale,' I said. 'I'll tell you about it perhaps, one day.'

'Pippa has told me a good deal,' said Bruce. 'I wish I'd known before. I might have been more helpful. I blame myself!'

'Don't,' I said, surprised that Pippa had talked to him

about me. 'Looking back doesn't work.'

'You're right there.'

'And guilt's no good either. How's Mandy?'

'Wonderful.'

'And you?'

'Wonderful too.'

We were both silent with our thoughts, then he said, 'Have you got your eye on somewhere else to live?'

'Yes. I've seen a house near Vauxhall Bridge. The street is alive with MPs, and only just going up market, so it's reasonable. They're very pretty old houses. Regency. Nicely proportioned rooms and small gardens down wrought-iron stairs. Not bijou, but not big. Should be fine.'

'I like the sound of it.'

'Good. Perhaps you could come round one day, you and Mandy. It would be lovely to see you.'

'Thanks. I'll ask Mandy.'

'When I've settled in,' I said, '- and that's if I can sell this and buy that!'

'Quite! Thanks for ringing, darling.'

'Lovely to hear your voice,' I said. And when he'd hung up, I burst into tears.

It had been marvellous to speak to him though, and he really had sounded happy enough, which was a relief as I'd been hearing rumours that he and Mandy weren't getting on too well.

One day soon after, Pippa rang me in great excitement.

'Guess what! Mandy's having a baby - I shall have a little brother or sister at last!'

I felt winded but said how delighted I was and asked how Bruce and Mandy felt about it.

'Over the moon!' said Pippa. 'It's quite a turn up, isn't it?'

'It is indeed,' I said. 'I'll give Mandy a ring.'

'D'you think that's wise?' asked Pippa.

142

'Well of course,' I replied. 'Why shouldn't it be?'

'I think she's still a bit jealous of you,' said Pippa.

'Oh rubbish, darling,' I said. 'How could she be? Bruce is married to her now, and she's young and I'm old.'

'You don't look particularly old,' said Pippa, and I thought she sounded faintly disapproving.

'Well I feel it!' I retorted. 'She has nothing to fear from me.'

I telephoned Mandy. She sounded slightly cold and distant, but doggedly polite.

'I'm so glad for you,' I said, 'and Bruce must be thrilled to bits.'

'Yes,' she said. 'He's as chuffed as hell.'

'D'you mind if it's a boy or a girl?' I asked.

'Not at all,' she said, 'as long as it is a perfect baby and not deformed in any way.'

'I'm sure it will be perfect,' I said. 'Give my love to Bruce and congratulate him for me, won't you?'

'Certainly,' she said.

'And do come and visit me one day. It would be great fun to see you both again.'

'Thanks,' she said. 'We'll do that very thing.'

I didn't think she would, and I was right, but the next few months were so fully occupied with selling the Chelsea house and buying the new one and putting it into shape, that I didn't mind too much.

The baby was born three days after I had settled in, and was a boy. Bruce had always dreamed of having a boy. I thought of ringing them again, decided against it, and wrote them both a letter, which Bruce answered with a short friendly note. No invitation to see them, and no suggestion of visiting me; and just a PS to say he hoped the new house was what I wanted.

I had a blow-by-blow description of the confinement and baby from Pippa, who never failed to give me news of him

143

whenever she communicated. He sounded a splendid little chap, and of course I wished I could see him. Bruce's son.

I suppose it was Mandy, the baby, and my feeling of exclusion that precipitated me into my love affair with Tony Bingham. I was lonely and feeling my age, and he was young, attractive, and a great ego-booster; but it turned Pippa away from me again completely. I couldn't see why. She was very angry, and told me that she thought at my age I'd have better things to do! This struck me as so funny and so absurd that I wanted her to laugh at herself with me, but she was far too upset.

'You said you were feeling old the other day,' she said. 'Doesn't it strike you as rather undignified to have an affair with a mere boy at your age?'

I was reminded of Hermione Baddeley's line in a revue I had seen years ago – 'There's nothing mere about a boy' – but said only a little hysterically that I didn't think dignity had all that much to do with affairs, and that at thirty-five Tony was hardly a boy.

'But half your age, Mother.'

'A lot younger, certainly. But I'm not yet seventy!'

'It can't work,' she said.

'Mandy is years younger than Bruce and you raised no objection to that business,' I said. 'In fact you rather encouraged it, if I remember rightly.'

'Daddy is a man,' she said, portentously.

'I did discover that,' I said dryly, 'but I don't see why middle-aged men are almost expected to have affairs with young women, and middle-aged women aren't. It's nonsensical.'

'Don't be silly, Mother,' she said furiously. 'You know perfectly well it's an entirely different thing.'

'I know nothing of the sort,' I said. 'Every affair, indeed

144

every relationship, has the possibility of failure or success. Age isn't the only difficulty along the line, by a long chalk.'

'What do you suppose people will think?' she demanded.

'As Tony is almost too good-looking to be true, they'll probably think I'm extremely lucky,' I replied.

'I see you're in one of your obstinate moods,' said Pippa, 'so there's no reasoning with you, but I want you to know that I'm really very shocked. I suppose he's queer.'

'He shows no signs of it,' I said.

'Well, you being so much older.'

'It's possible,' I said. 'Mother-dominated, perhaps. Just as Mandy was looking for a father?'

'If you'll forgive me, Mother,' she said, 'I think we'd better stop this conversation. It's making me feel rather sick. I suppose it has never occurred to you that you are making things very difficult for Charles and me?'

'No,' I said. 'How's that?'

'People will think you're a bit of a tramp. Sorry, Ma, but it's the truth.'

'Do they think your father is a tramp for marrying Mandy – or rather, did they when he was just living with her?'

'Of course not!' Pippa was contemptuous. 'Sometimes I think you have very odd ideas, Mother. You should try to live in the real world.'

'You don't quite know what you've said, darling,' I laughed, 'but yes, I agree I must live in the real world, and Tony is part of it. I need companionship, even at my age. I need love and affection. And because I've always had it, I need someone to depend on.'

'You've been a bit spoilt, haven't you, Mother?'

'See who's talking!' I rejoined, mildly.

'Mother!' Pippa was exasperated. 'I'm young, and I'm just starting on my life! You've had your day.'

'In your eyes, darling, that may well be true. In mine, since I'm still alive, I don't agree.'

'Are we to look forward to a succession of lovers?' She was being sarcastic now.

'I've no idea how life will turn out,' I said, 'but Tony is for now, and I'm touched and grateful that he should want me.'

'Then there's no more to be said,' she said, and hung up.

My affair with Tony was a sweet interlude, and I valued the experience more than I can say. He's a charming young man, clever, sophisticated and funny, and above all he has the capacity for tenderness. It lasted a long while, and now it is over we are still friends. It was primarily a physical relationship, and it came at a time when my need for someone close was very great.

At first all was well, except that I had a second recurring dream connected with Philip. In this one Philip was very young, and we floated along hand in hand across green meadows, and fields of corn and poppies. Little hedges divided the fields, and the sun shone warmly, and just before we came to earth Philip kissed me, and I awoke in a haze of happiness. It was a lovely dream, but I didn't want to be reminded of Philip just now, and was sad that it wasn't Tony with whom I was floating so blissfully. All the same, it was better than dreaming of Philip shooting himself: that was only an occasional waking nightmare.

Sex is on the whole a fairly narcissistic business, I suppose. A good deal of the 'I love you' that we murmur also contains 'I love me', and when we are ageing this is harder to do. Physically we are losing shape, however carefully we have looked after ourselves, and this in a sexual affair is disconcerting ... at least I found it so. I also found ageing bewildering. In many ways I was and am fascinated by the process, though I will hate losing my faculties, and have many fears about the unpleasant surprises that the gods may have in store for me – let alone how I'm going to die, which sometimes, unexpectedly, feels quite near. But I am glad that

146

I am no longer shy and no longer care so passionately what people think of me; on the contrary, I now care much more what I think of them. I am glad to know who I am; to have achieved many good friendships, to have made my way in the world successfully enough to have some sort of position (identity, if you like) and that I can also run my home well and efficiently. I regret that the ease with which I used to get my own way with men simply by looking helpless is over, that there were many more good parts for me as a young actress than there are now when experience has made me better at my job, and I dislike the knowledge that many people find it dull talking to an older woman. I don't enjoy losing my looks and my figure – 'But your face is so full of character!' I'm told. Is my neck full of character now that my jaw line is blurring, and there are rings round it? My eyes seem to be smaller too and there are lines round my mouth, and not only laugh lines! I'm plumper than I want to be, but daren't diet too much in case my face gets haggard. I can't wear short-sleeved dresses any more. Under my breasts the muscles have sagged, and on my upper legs too. More will happen in my sixties and seventies. Yet Tony loved me, and really loved me physically, which was a miracle for me; and every age is absorbingly interesting, if one finds any age in life absorbingly interesting! Mentally, too, it's good for a woman to be older, as men aren't frightened of an older woman being clever. This is a sad reflection on men, but it's a fact.

Before Tony goes out of this story, I should like to describe him a little. He is quite unlike either Philip or Bruce. He is of medium height, with mouse-coloured rather lanky hair worn a little long, and he has protuberant eyes, a neat nose and an amused sort of smile. This doesn't sound as if he's handsome, but he is. He is very attractive to women because he is a good listener, and few men listen to women. He is also very funny – a wonderful raconteur – and has an original mind. He's an actor, and although he is a good one, I think he will turn to

147

writing in the end. He has a writer's mentality, and I should know, having been married to Bruce for so long.

When we were on our own we got on marvellously. We have the same sense of humour, the same taste in houses, furniture, pictures, reading, and playgoing. Sex between us was really good. The difficulty was, as Pippa (and nearly anyone else who saw us together) predicted, that the age difference showed itself in our friends, and in our levels of tolerance. Tony, like most of his generation, loves noise. Loud music blaring most of the day, screaming parties, and dancing at discos to noise of a decibel level so extreme that it hurts my eardrums. He is also desperately untidy. Pippa is so tidy that it worries me, but Tony is so untidy that he can turn anywhere into a slum in twenty minutes. Naturally his friends are young, and mine on the whole are middle-aged. Holidays were difficult because the friends he made in the South of France and Italy and elsewhere treated me as a relic from an incomprehensible past, and I found their conversation a touch on the boring side. It couldn't last and it didn't, but he saw me through a very difficult period, and without him life would have been the poorer. When he came to me, I'd lost my nerve about myself. By the time he had left, I was on course again.

He went to a younger girl, and that hasn't lasted either, but he'll find himself one day perhaps, and good luck to him.

I say that my life was on course. I'm speaking strictly in the personal sense. As an actress it was getting harder to keep going.

In a good many ways, women's careers are more complicated than men's. Never more so than in acting. The ratio of women's parts to men's is one to eight, and women's ages matter a good deal more than men's. For a girl, there are the juvenile parts to play: sullen and withdrawn, or pretty and lovable. Next come the leading ladies, the big star parts which need breadth and style; some women fail as early as this transition. Then come the mothers, the career women, the Aunt parts, and the eccentrics. Lastly come the real character parts, but far fewer parts are written for women at this age, and this was the area which I was now reaching. Although I kept going, and was always surprised at my good fortune, I also had regrets that I hadn't made more of my time when I was young. I should have gone for the classics, because they are the only way in which one can measure oneself against the past and the future, and they are much more rewarding to play. How sad that one only has one life!

All the same, by the time Tony left me I had increased my circle of friends, and I wasn't lonely any more.

I missed Philip. I missed Tony. Above all I missed Bruce. But I could manage, and manage well as a single woman.

CHAPTER NINETEEN

I was on a British Council tour in Turkey when I next heard from Pippa. She was pregnant, and seemed delighted. She wanted to know when I should be home, as she longed to see me again. She also said that she hoped I wasn't missing Tony (she hated to say she had told me so), and that I should have let her know he had left me, as she and Charles would have loved to see me. Charles was doing so well that she hadn't seen too much of him lately, but he was as excited as she was that they were going to have a baby.

It was a long, chatty, affectionate letter, but something about it made me uneasy. I came to the conclusion that it must be because Pippa was feeling uneasy, too. This was very unlike her, and I wondered what was troubling her. Charles?

I wrote at once to say how happy I was about the baby, and how I longed to be back with her. We still had five more weeks on tour I said, but I would telephone her on the night of my return.

I was enjoying the tour. I was playing Mrs Malaprop in *The Rivals* – a good part in a splendid play. It was spring everywhere we went: in England it had been cold, but in Brussels (where we ate wonderful sea-food in the little lanes behind La Grande Place) the sun shone all day. In Belgrade, flowering trees lined the streets (though nothing could lift my depression in that sad and shabby city). Paris was its own magnificent, chic, exciting self; in Athens, the roses were rioting; in Istanbul, the Bosphorus was already blue. And

Geneva, Copenhagen, Stockholm, and Oslo were still to come.

My two great friends in the cast were a couple of homosexuals. They were funny, bitchy and full of curiosity and gossip. They had great taste, took an enormous interest in my clothes, loved food – and adored sightseeing. I was the right age for them to be interested in me, and in their company the days flew by.

Until Pippa's letter I had been happy. From then on I was worried. I wondered what was the matter with her. Whatever it was, had she told Bruce about it? To think, I'd be a grandmother soon! What fun! And Bruce a grandfather and father in the space of three years! Would I have to see something of Bruce now? Did I want to? Yes, I did.

Very surprisingly, Pippa came to Heathrow to meet me on my return. She looked in blooming health, hardly any sign of the baby yet, but she spoke too fast, and nervously.

'I've got some lunch for you at home,' she said. 'Will you come? I want to show you all my preparations for the child.'

'Of course I'll come. I'm so thrilled for you, my darling. I so hope that you are happy, too.'

'Yes, of course. Of course we want it to be a boy.'

'What a shame!' I laughed. 'We were delighted when we had you!'

'Were you? I should have thought you would have wanted a boy.' She stared at me for a moment, with her chin held slightly defiantly. 'I often wished I were one for Daddy's sake.'

'Oh, what nonsense!' I exclaimed. 'I've never seen a more feminine little girl!'

'Well, I couldn't help that!'

'And Bruce doted on you for it!'

Her face clouded.

151

'How is he?' I asked. 'And Mandy? And the boy? I would so love to see him. Does he look like Bruce?'

'They're fine, and yes, little Reggie looks like Daddy.' She sounded off-hand, almost brusque, and I looked at her in surprise.

'You don't sound very certain,' I said.

'I'm perfectly certain they're well,' she said.

'Then what?' I asked.

'There's a bit more gossip, but I'm sure there's nothing in it.'

'What sort of gossip?'

'Oh, nothing.'

'Come on, darling. Don't be silly. I'm old enough to be told things by this time. What sort of gossip?'

'There are rumours that Mandy has a boyfriend.'

'Oh dear!' I exclaimed. 'Is it serious?'

'I don't know. But I naturally don't like it, for Daddy's sake.'

'He can take care of himself,' I said, with more conviction than I felt.

'He certainly had to in the past, Mother, but I had hoped that had all changed.' Her face was set as she stared through the windscreen. It began to rain and she switched on the wipers which whirred monotonously. 'Poor Daddy! I wonder why it is.'

'Why what is?' I asked, though I well knew what she was going to say.

'Why he falls for the sort of woman who will play him up – sorry, Mother, but you know what I mean!'

'I wasn't in the least the sort of woman who would play him up!' I retorted, nettled in spite of myself. 'I thought I had explained to you about Philip, and he was the only lover I ever had apart from your father – until the divorce. Mandy is different. She is very young, and he's much older. I suppose she wants someone of her own age.'

'I wouldn't if I were married to a wonderful man like Daddy. He's terribly good-looking still, and he's brilliantly clever, and she'll never find anyone else like him if she searches the world over.'

'That's true, but as I say, she's very young.'

'I wish I weren't his daughter, then I could have married him myself.' She laughed self-consciously. 'That's a joke.'

'How's Charles?' I asked, to change the subject.

Her mouth hardened. 'Fine.'

'You said he was getting on very well in business. I'm so glad.'

'Yes, but it seems to mean that we don't see too much of each other at the moment. He flies all over the world and he never seems to be able to take me, although lots of business-men do take their wives, and when he gets back and I've been doing boring old nothing in this vile climate, all he wants to do is to stay at home.'

'Darling, don't!' I exclaimed anxiously. 'Lots of wives do it, and it always ends in tears.'

'Do what?'

'The wives envy their businessmen husbands their wonder-ful life-style without understanding how exhausting travel and success can be.'

'You must admit it must be marvellous to see all those places!'

'I'm sure you will too, one day,' I soothed.

'Daddy was a huge success, but he and you spent most of your time together,' said Pippa sulkily.

'Well, just now isn't the moment to want to go travelling, is it? The baby is going to need all your attention for a bit.'

'Yes,' said Pippa, 'I know.' She didn't sound particularly pleased.

Once inside her home she cheered up and began showing me the rooms she had started to decorate for the baby and the nurse.

'I haven't made the nursery too whimsy,' she said. 'Baby talk and Winnie the Pooh and all that are fairly stultifying, don't you think?'

'Rather early to worry about that,' I laughed.

'Never too early, I'm sure. There are six months to go, which is only twenty-four weeks, so I'm getting ahead with the knitting and sewing – I'll show you. And I've ordered the pram and a pretty wonderful cot. I've rather gone to town on that.'

'It's lovely that Charles is so happy about the baby.'

'Yes. In fact he's keener than I am.'

'I thought you were thrilled.'

'I'm a bit scared too.'

'I'm sure there's nothing to be scared about. The doctor says all is well, doesn't he?' I was suddenly worried.

'Yes. The doctor's a she by the way, and she says I'm in excellent shape. But I want you to tell me what I've got to go through, and give me tips and so on, and I want you to help me about living as normal a life as possible afterwards. I'm enjoying life at the moment, and I don't want to be bogged down.'

'Darling,' I said, 'you're a capable girl. If I could live a fairly normal life after you came, I'm sure you'll be able to manage it.'

She looked at me sideways, opened her mouth to say something, thought better of it, then murmured, 'You've always known where you were going.'

This was so ludicrously inaccurate that I said, 'You couldn't be further from the truth. I thought you had realised how absurdly badly I have managed my life.'

'I think you've managed rather well,' she said dryly, and I realised that a lifetime's jealousy still precluded any real understanding between us.

On an impulse I said, 'What do you think of Mandy now? I mean, now that she may have got a boyfriend and be cheating on your father?'

'I don't like her as much as I did, naturally,' she said. 'But at least she's keeping him in touch with a young world.'

'Yes,' I said. 'Like Tony with me.'

She drew down the corners of her mouth, and said, 'Do you see him now?'

'Oh, yes,' I said. 'Luckily we're still good friends.'

We had lunch together then, but after she drove me home I felt depressed and drained.

The baby, a boy, arrived exactly on time. He weighed eight pounds, and had a vestige of hair. They decided to name him Henry. He was a beautiful baby, and I fell in love with him at once.

Bruce was at the hospital when I arrived. He looked a bit drawn, I thought, and we didn't seem to have much to say to one another, but he seemed pleased to see me, and his icily cold manner had completely thawed; in fact, as he had when I telephoned, he put himself out to charm.

The christening was a grand affair. My parents were there, but I thought my father looked ill.

Since the divorce I had been seeing quite a lot of them. My father's successor had been given a smaller, modern house, and Daddy was allowed to stay in our old house until he died. It was nice going home and being spoilt, and I must say that, although the place was as untidy and erratically run as it always had been, my mother certainly hadn't lost her touch for making it a happy sort of haven – a great gift. Being there in my old room again brought back magical memories of childhood, but it also reminded me of the holiday when I had first met Granny Godsend, and was falling in love with Philip . . .

Now, seeing how pale and drawn my father looked I suspected that he might not last much longer, and the thought made me infinitely sad.

CHAPTER TWENTY

Before very long Pippa had a second child, a daughter, whom she called Amanda. She and Charles still stayed together, although there were obvious stresses and strains, and she remained as fanatically houseproud as ever. She brought the children up strictly and well. They were always very clean, very well-behaved, and beautifully dressed; in fact I sometimes privately thought them too perfect, as unchildish as Pippa had been – almost like little mannequins. However, it was none of my business. Pippa had become very silent, almost morose; but she no longer complained that Charles left her behind when he went on his travels although she was still a very beautiful woman.

I now saw Bruce quite regularly, as he loved our grandchildren as much as I did. He was still with Mandy, who still, according to rumour, had a boyfriend in tow – a pop star. Poor Bruce! I began to see what Pippa had hinted at. It seemed a shame that his wives weren't faithful to him!

At this time I was working constantly. I did a lot of television, and became well-known in a way I hadn't been for several years. I liked the work very much, finding the new young directors sympathetic and able. The casts were predominantly young, and I liked being with them, although naturally my own age-group interested me the most. I also did a couple of tours on the dinner-theatre circuit – master-minded by that business-like and charming actor-comedian Derek Nimmo, who has made a new name for himself in this field.

Dinner-theatre, as Derek runs it, is unique – at least as far as the British theatre is concerned. For homesick expatriates languishing in comparative luxury all over the Near and Far East, the tours are a marvellous link with home: Cairo, Dubai, Abu Dhabi, Bahrein, Singapore, Jakarta, Kuala Lumpur, Papua New Guinea, Hong Kong, Thailand and, more recently, Peking – all these are visited. And it's a wonderful life for the actors, who are put up free at the five-star hotels where they play, and get a salary as well. The plays are farces or broad comedies because these are more likely to be enjoyed by the sort of people who have paid a great deal of money for a first-class dinner in a hotel ballroom.

What a strange life actors lead – not least because they can seldom control their own careers! They can say no to the worst offers if they can afford to, but although called 'self-employed' they are entirely dependent on the whims of others. Agents, casting directors and managers see them through their own eyes, and the offers the actors get are the result. The lucky few get the good plays and the classics, the rest get the balance of what is going. An acting life (when one is lucky enough to find work) is a succession of new jobs, new opportunities, new companies and casts, all starting and stopping at unpredictable moments. In each job in the unsubsidised theatre, in television plays and in radio, the performers are all 'new boys and girls'. Sometimes they know some of their colleagues, often they don't, which can be tiring as well as exhilarating. All I can say is that, for the time being, I was enjoying myself – enormously.

I had become completely used to living on my own, and was positively revelling in it. I was seldom lonely. My home, when I was there, was my joy, and it was pleasant not to have to consider anyone else's wishes about meals, going out, getting up early, or housekeeping if I didn't want to. I read a great deal, and I was coming to terms with age at last. Life wasn't so exciting, but it was absorbing. It was tranquil, and fulfilling. Who could ask for more? Except that I felt, once again, as I had when my affair with Philip had come to a standstill, that I was marking time. I couldn't believe that the calm would last.

The first thing to shatter it was that Mandy left Bruce, taking little Reggie with her. Her boyfriend had at last decided to marry her, and she was still in love with him. Bruce, it seemed, was not all that unhappy at losing her, but he did mind about his son. He didn't enjoy the prospect of a second divorce, but as he said when he telephoned to tell me about it, he had asked for trouble when he'd married someone so much younger than himself, and he had been lucky to have so many good years with her.

'She's a nice girl,' he said, 'and I hope she's going to be happy. Reggie is another matter. This business of having parents in two places, and a stepfather at home, never really works out well, and he's a dear little chap and deserves better. You were always telling me how guilty you felt about Philip, and sometimes it got me down, but now I'm the one who feels guilty, because if this marriage had worked, Reggie would still have the two of us! Now I understand what you went through.'

He sounded so down that I was tempted to ask him straight round to a meal, but I decided to let him make the running, because I didn't want him to think that I was waiting to fall into his arms. I wasn't – in fact I wasn't at all sure what I would do, in the unlikely event of his wanting to come back to me.

He telephoned again the following week, and rather hesitantly invited himself to dinner.

'Would that be too much of a sweat?' he asked. 'I wouldn't want you to go to any trouble over the food, but we could talk much more easily if we aren't in a restaurant besieged by waiters, and I have a lot I want to talk to you about.'

158

'It would be fine,' I replied, and we arranged for a night the following week (I was out of work at the time). 'I look forward to it.'

But things didn't pan out that way.

I had a call from my Aunt Bessie, to say that Mother had fallen down stairs and broken her hip. She was in the local hospital but would need help when she returned home. Aunt Bessie could stay with her later, but had arranged to visit friends for the next three weeks, so could I please go home?

Of course I could, and I did.

When Father had died sometime earlier, Mother had had to leave the rectory, as I knew she would. Together, we found her a small and pleasant house in the village, and she had managed surprisingly well on her own. She was well-loved and had many friends and helpers, and I still visited her as often as I could. Father's death had left her even more vague and distracted than before, but she had guts, and had kept right on with her good works.

I went to her new home, and tidied the place from top to bottom. I wouldn't have enjoyed this in my own place, but at Mother's I did. Nonetheless, she needed a lot of looking after when she came back from the hospital, even though we had a nurse to come in daily, and I began to worry about how she could keep going when I had to go back to London. I had reckoned without Aunt Bessie.

Aunt Bessie was short and squat, with a deep voice and thick legs. It was reputed that she had been extremely pretty as a young girl but there was no sign of it by this time. She had a little grey bristling moustache, small blue eyes, a hearty laugh and a ribald sense of humour. For a long time she had lived in Bournemouth with a woman friend called 'Harry' Larkin. She wore trousers and a tie, and when she went out she wore a battered man's hat with a couple of fishing flies hooked onto the crown. She was as practical as a man about the house, but she disliked housework, although she was a good cook. She and Mother had never been close, as from the start they were totally unalike. They had quarrelled fiercely as children and had hardly bothered to see each other since, but now in their old age they seemed to have come to terms with one another. They spent hours recalling the past, and in a curious way they complemented each other, my mother being so feminine and Aunt Bessie so masculine! The long and the short of it was that Aunt Bessie offered to share a household with Mother in whichever home she would prefer and Mother chose her own. This left Aunt Bessie with a move on her hands, but with great plans for the future.

'I've been lonely since old Harry died,' she said to me happily, 'and I'm looking forward to a new life. I don't think Josie and I will get on one another's nerves. We've got just enough in common, and I like looking after people. The fact that we're to share your mother's house will probably keep me in my proper place, too. I'm a bit of a bossy boots by nature. As it happens, I prefer this house to mine. Old Harry had modern tastes and I let her have her way, but I really prefer old houses and old furniture. I'm going to buy a half-share in this one with the money from the sale of mine, so we'll both be better off.'

I left for London feeling happier.

Bruce rang on the night I returned. After asking after my mother, he said, 'What about that dinner you promised me, darling? Is it still on?'

'If you'd like it to be.'

'I would. Very much.'

The evening went off pleasantly until nearly the end. I began by being on my guard against him, because it was all too easy to slip back into accepting him as a part of the domestic scenery. He was still astonishingly good to look at. Rugged men have the advantage that age-lines, for some

160

considerable time, only add to their attractions; and he hadn't put on weight. He was also, as he had always been, a good talker – and very funny too, when he wanted to be. I had managed to make a delicious meal (he was right, I had indeed sweated over it) and I had chosen the wines with considerable care. I'm not sure at this point why I had gone to so much trouble; whether I hoped to ensnare him again with my new housewifely accomplishments (since my nerves had completely gone about my looks) – in other words, whether it was vanity which had inspired me – or a feminist wish to show him how well I could do without him. Anyway, the result was encouraging. We talked effortlessly and enjoyed one another's company.

He hadn't changed much, it seemed, and I liked being with someone whom I knew too well for us to have to go to the bother of sending and reading smoke signals. We were comfortable, and we fitted.

After dinner, and over liqueurs, he began doing what I had hoped and feared he would; telling me how much he missed me, and what a fool he had been to leave me.

Finally he said, 'That damned visit to Suffolk was the last straw! And of course I was very attracted to Mandy. I won't say a word against her – I was far too old for her, and after the first few years it showed. For both of us. Her friends were all young, and a lot of them were bright and amusing, but few of them had what I call weight. I came to feel an outsider in my own home. What's more, now that young Reggie is with his mother most of the time (and she has a pretty crazy bunch around her), I can't wholeheartedly put my foot down, because I'm really old enough to be his grandfather.'

'I fully accept that I shouldn't have gone to Suffolk,' I said, 'but I did write a letter, and I apologised, and asked you to try and understand. Come to that, I pretty well bared my soul, but you didn't bother to answer.'

161

'What are you talking about?' asked Bruce. 'I don't remember any letter.'

'I left a letter on the hall table for you to read while I was with Philip and Mary,' I said. 'I begged you to wait until the visit was over before you threw our marriage away and I swore to finish with Philip once and for all.'

'There was no letter on the hall table,' said Bruce. 'I thought, being an idiot, that there might be, so I especially looked to see. There was nothing.'

'That's absurd!' I replied quite heatedly. 'I know I left it there. I checked and double-checked before I left. Oh! ...' To my horror, I had suddenly remembered Pippa's face at the drawing-room window, and her furtive disappearance from sight behind the curtain.

'Oh what?' asked Bruce, and I could see that, in spite of himself and the image he wanted to produce, he was feeling belligerent.

I hesitated. It had all happened so long ago. Was it worth trying to justify the past? On the other hand, if we didn't get this straight now there wasn't going to be much future between Bruce and me.

'Well?' he insisted.

I didn't want to let Pippa down. On the other hand, if the matter was as important as it seemed to Bruce, I wasn't being fair to him. 'Try not to be angry,' I said slowly. 'The past is the past and we all of us had problems very different from those we have today.'

'So?'

'I may be very wrong about this, and if I am, I'm being damnably unfair, but just before I left, when I was in the car, I happened to look up, and I saw ...'

'Pippa!' interrupted Bruce furiously. 'My God – the little so and so! What happened?'

With reluctance I told him what I had seen. 'But it doesn't necessarily mean she took the letter,' I said. 'Anyway, darling, what's the point of fussing about it, now? What's done is done. And if it hadn't been the letter, it might well have been something else, the way you were feeling then!'

'I'm going to find out about that letter,' said Bruce, 'if it's the last thing I do.'

'Why?' I asked. 'Can't we let things be? I'm glad we've had this conversation, though, because I always thought it was rather cruel of you never to say a word.'

'I was horribly hurt,' said Bruce. 'I went through hell and Pippa knew it, and she always pretended to love me so much. How *could* she?'

'She was jealous,' I said. 'She has always been jealous of me. You know she has, and she always will be. But she and I get on far better these days and I'd love to keep it that way. It may be, too, that she quite honestly saw you as younger than me, in spirit, and genuinely thought that Mandy would be better for you.'

'Then she should have minded her own bloody business!' said Bruce angrily. 'No one should play God with other people's lives.'

'We really do all make mistakes, darling,' I said, anxiously.

'To try to split up the marriage between your own mother and father seems pretty sick to me,' said Bruce. He ran a hand through his thick hair. 'Blast her! Blast her! Blast her! You wait till I see her!'

'Leave it,' I said. I tried to change the subject. 'Tell me more about the new play. You said that Duncan Weldon is going to put it on. Have you got the London theatre yet?'

'Probably the Duke of York's,' he said.

'About perfect, by the sound of it.'

'Should be,' he agreed.

'Got a director, or any of the cast?'

'Alan Mortimer is going to direct, and Gwen Madge is going to be in it.'

'Sounds promising. And where are you going to live?'

'At least Mandy isn't turning me out of the house,' said Bruce. 'Lenny is as rich as Croesus – a pad in London, a farm in Sussex with the obligatory swimming pool, and a place in Spain. As pop singers go, he's not a bad chap. As you can imagine, in the early stages I was always being dragged off to see him, and he's got talent. I just don't like the thought of young Reggie being brought up among that crowd, though. He's such a winner.'

This thought seemed to depress him again, and fairly soon he left.

He kissed me on both cheeks before he went. 'Darling June, I can't tell you what this evening has done for me! I've been happier than I've been for so long. May we go out together one evening soon? The very best restaurant this time?'

'I'd love it,' I replied.

CHAPTER TWENTY-ONE

Pippa was on the telephone, and she sounded hysterical.

'How could you?' she sobbed. 'How could you, after all this time!'

'How could I what?'

'How could you tell Daddy that I stole your letter to him all those years ago?'

'Well, didn't you?' I asked.

'I thought I was doing it for the best! ...' Her voice sounded desperate.

'That's what I told your father.'

'He's furious. He says he doesn't want to see me again.'

'That's nonsense of course,' I said. 'He'll come round.'

'He says he never wanted to leave you, and that I've ruined his life!'

'He's going through a bad patch,' I said, 'what with Mandy leaving him, and worries about young Reggie.'

'He's far too old for Reggie, Mother! It's much better for the boy to be with Mandy,' said Pippa.

'Your poor father knows that, but it's one of the problems of marrying someone so much younger, isn't it? And he doesn't like Mandy's set.'

'Don't! I feel simply awful!' exclaimed Pippa. 'How was I to know she'd fall in love with a pop star? Lenny's so crass! So ugh! And so dead-end boring!'

'Do you feel awful because Bruce is angry, or because you're sorry about stealing my letter?' I asked grimly.

'You should have heard him!' cried Pippa. 'I can't bear Daddy to feel like this about me! We've always been so much more than father and daughter.'

'Exactly,' I said. 'That's one of the things that went wrong in our family. Perhaps what has happened is a good thing. It's forcing us to take a fresh look at ourselves. Of course Bruce will want to see you again, but this hang-up between you has to stop sometime if you're ever going to grow up – and you'll have to, difficult though it is. We all have to.'

'I knew you wouldn't be sympathetic. I told Daddy so,' said Pippa.

'And what did he say?' I asked.

'He said, why the hell should you be?'

'Ah! What do you think about that as an answer?'

'Sorry?'

'I said what do you think about that as an answer?'

'I don't understand it,' said Pippa.

'Well, you try,' I said. I found that I was very angry indeed, and was surprised at myself for it.

'I don't know what to do!' moaned Pippa. 'And I'm so miserable at the moment!'

'I can't help you, I'm afraid,' I said coldly.

'I don't only mean about Daddy,' she said. 'I'm worried about Charles, too.'

'About Charles?' I was immediately on her side.

'Yes. I don't quite know what's wrong, but there's something. He's behaving quite differently towards me. He's coming back awfully late at night, and he's going away far more often, and not always abroad apparently. Do you remember Marcia Donald?'

'A dark, horsy woman?' I asked. 'Long black hair, deep voice, high colouring, and rather handsome?'

'That's the one. He's been spending several weekends with her when I've thought he was on business trips. Angela

166

Thornton told me. She's seen them together and thought she'd better warn me.'

'Very kind of her,' I said dryly. 'Have you talked to Charles about it?'

'Yes, I have, and he denies it. He says he was staying with his boss nearby, and that his boss and Marcia are friends.'

'That's OK then, isn't it?'

'I wish it were. I'd believe it if I could, but Angela swears he's staying with *Marcia*! He's acting so strangely altogether, and he's turning the children against me, too.'

'Look,' I said. 'Come to lunch and let's talk it over.'

She came, and she looked terrible. For the first time in her life she didn't seem to have taken the smallest trouble with her appearance. She was wearing a hideous dress, and looked as if she hadn't seen the inside of a hairdresser's for months. She was very thin, and her voice was sharp and on the edge of tears.

'Darling child!' I exclaimed. 'This is no good at all if you want to keep a straying husband! You really must pull yourself together! Just look at you!'

'Daddy is so furious that he won't even answer the telephone,' said Pippa. 'I tried to talk to him about Charles, but he hung up. He absolutely hates me!'

'Of course he doesn't!' I said. 'It's given him a shock, that's all. Now tell me about Charles.'

'Why *now*? Why did you have to tell Daddy *now*?'

'It just came out,' I answered helplessly. 'Come on, darling – about Charles.'

'But it's all so long ago ...' she said tearfully.

'I know,' I replied. 'And I suppose it does seem unfair that you should be found out after so long, but has it sunk in how much harm you did? Your father says he has been through hell.'

'You put him through hell yourself, always mooning about Philip! All my childhood you made him miserable. You didn't take care of him, and you didn't take care of me!'

I was exasperated. 'Are we going to talk about Charles or aren't we?' I demanded. 'If you want my help, don't attack me. I may have done all the things you accuse me of, I may be wickedness itself, but just at the moment your own hands aren't very clean. Bruce is angry because you cheated on us. I'm less upset because I'm used to feeling an outsider in your world. But, by God, if I have to listen to much more of this stuff, Pippa, I'll be as angry as he is! You're a married woman. You have a glamorous husband whom you seem to be afraid of losing, and two enchanting children. You have money, position, a nice house, and until now doting parents. You've been pampered and spoilt all your life, and now we've discovered that you behaved very badly indeed to both of us. Stop this self-pity at once, and for a start, apologise to me! I invited you here to try to help about you and Charles, but if you're going to go on like this, I shall have to ask you to go. What I did about Philip is your father's and my affair. Not yours. So do you want to talk about Charles, or not?'

'Yes.'

'Good. So where's that apology?'

She was silent.

'Well?' I asked.

She still said nothing.

'Very well,' I said, 'that's enough! I'm sorry you're having a rough time, but if you've behaved towards Charles in anything like the way you have behaved towards me all your life, you've brought it on yourself, and you'll have to deal with it without my help. So on your bike, darling, until you come to your senses.'

'I told Daddy you wouldn't help.' She had put on her little-girl-lost look, but this time it didn't melt my heart.

She fiddled about with the sherry I had poured out for her, drank it, fiddled some more with her handbag, then made for the door. 'Goodbye,' she said. 'Be seeing you.'

I didn't reply.

'The children will miss you,' she said.

'I'll miss them,' I answered.

She stayed by the door, but she didn't open it, and I said nothing. Finally she said in a small voice, 'I'm sorry, Mummy.'

'Good,' I said, briskly.

She still stood by the door. 'So may I come back in and have lunch and talk about Charles?'

'Of course.'

From what she had told me, it did indeed look as if Charles was playing the field, but as I didn't know his side of the story, I wasn't sure what advice to give. I was certain that he was a loving father, and I knew from my own experience that although Bruce had been attracted to Mandy for some time before he left me, he hadn't actually wanted to go. I suggested carefully to Pippa that it might be the same with Charles. 'Have another talk with him,' I said. 'Don't be self-righteous with him, or lose your temper, and try to understand his point of view. If people stray it's usually because we have failed them in some way. I know I failed. Try to understand how you've failed.'

She rang me a few days later, obviously feeling better. 'I've talked to Charles,' she said, 'and he says he *does* run into Marcia at his boss's house, and he is attracted, but that it's nothing to worry about. He says he has no intention of leaving me! Isn't that marvellous? And even better, Daddy seems to have forgiven me! I told him I had apologised to you, and we're back on our usual footing again.'

I pretended more relief than I felt. I didn't share Pippa's faith in Charles's protestations about Marcia, for one thing; and I was bothered by Pippa's emphasis on patching things up with her father – as if that were more important even than her future with Charles. What an obsessive she was – what obsessives we both were.

*   *   *

Bruce dropped by and took me out to dinner.

He was still very upset about Pippa. He hadn't forgiven her, whatever she thought, and I had the greatest difficulty in making him understand that at least some of the blame for her behaviour was ours. I had actively encouraged her fixation on Bruce, through guilt, and Bruce had certainly not discouraged it.

Bruce looked thoughtful.

'Charles is a decent fellow. I wish we knew what was going wrong,' he said.

'Well we don't, and we mustn't interfere,' I replied.

'Do you think that her passion for me has something to do with it?' he asked.

'Her passion for you is, consciously or unconsciously, at the back of everything she does,' I said, amazed that I could at last be saying this.

From then on, we saw each other regularly, and we visited Pippa in her beautiful tidy house. Neither Charles nor the children were there very often, and she seemed rather lonely; but when I said so, she flared out at me and said she liked it that way. She said she didn't want her children to miss out on any fun that might be going. She said she remembered only too well what it was like being an only child, and being tied to the house so much. Then she said, 'You and Daddy are getting back together again, I hear. Is that true?'

My heart sank, but I answered evenly, 'We're seeing a good deal of one another at the moment, yes.'

'Is that wise?' she asked.

'For whom?' I asked.

She looked rather confused, and muttered, 'I mean you've left each other once. Is it wise to start all over again?'

'We'll see,' I said.

She pursed her lips. 'Are you thinking of marrying again?'

'I certainly am, and I suspect he is, but we haven't actually discussed it, let alone come to a decision.' I smiled wryly. 'We'll let you know when we do.'

She didn't like this.

I considered her. 'Tell me,' I said, 'would you like it if we did?'

'If it were for the best,' she answered primly.

You are a pompous child, I thought.

'That's what we're trying to decide,' I said. 'And if it did make us happy, would it make *you* happy?'

'Of course,' she said, but she flushed.

'I hope so,' I said, 'but I rather doubt it. I think I had better tell you straight out, Pippa, that I am getting heartily sick of your everlasting hostility. One day you'll go too far, and then if Bruce and I do get together again, it will be you who will be out in the cold, where you have tried to put me ever since I can remember.'

She looked shocked. 'Mother, that's not true!' she exclaimed.

'You often call your father Daddy, but me, almost always Mother . . . more formal, don't you think?'

'I always have,' she blustered.

'Quite.'

'You see, it is Daddy who has always loved me.'

'We have both always loved you, but I'm beginning to be discouraged,' I said.

I felt bad saying such things while she did indeed have problems, but it had to be said some time, and there were problems for Bruce and me, too.

CHAPTER TWENTY-TWO

One Saturday night, after a very happy day spent in one another's company, Bruce and I slept together. After that it was only a matter of time before he moved in, although we were still undecided about marriage. In case things didn't work out after all, Bruce kept on his house. It was a good idea to have an office away from home anyway, and it left us room for manoeuvre. It was Bruce who told Pippa about it, and to my amazement she seemed genuinely delighted. Her problems seemed to be stable for the moment, and she sounded serene.

Bruce's new play was still doing big business at the Duke of York's, and now it was sold to America.

'I'll have to go,' he said. 'Come with me, and we'll get married over there.'

'I've accepted the BBC television series,' I said, 'so I can't. I wish I could.'

'You mean it?'

'Yes.'

'About America, or marriage?'

'Certainly about America.'

'And marriage?'

I hesitated. 'We're very happy as we are, surely? Why bother to re-marry?'

'I grudge every moment we've been unmarried,' he said. 'I want us to be a unit again.'

I laughed. 'Aren't we a unit, as you call it, now?'

172

'Not in my terms. It matters to me,' he said earnestly. 'It really does.'

'It took me ages to learn to live on my own,' I said, a little ruefully. 'I don't want to think of them as wasted years.'

'In some ways, most of us waste all our years,' said Bruce.

'Oh, very philosophical!' I replied, cheerfully.

'It's true as far as I'm concerned,' said Bruce seriously. 'Except for my work – I haven't wasted my time there.'

'I've wasted mine even about work,' I said, and suddenly felt depressed.

'So marry me, darling,' said Bruce. 'Don't let's waste more.'

'You're going to America, I'm going into a television series. If we marry now, we shan't have time for a honeymoon. If you still feel like marriage after your return, then let's marry as soon as I've finished my TV stint, OK? We didn't have a honeymoon last time, if you remember. Can we have one this?'

'You bet!'

'I finish in November. Could we go to the Caribbean like Pippa and Charles? I've always wanted to.'

'Anywhere you like!' He looked heartbreakingly young and eager.

'We have to tell Pippa,' I said.

'We'll tell her in November,' replied Bruce, firmly.

Aunt Bessie rang to say that Mother was ailing. 'I'm not quite sure what's the matter. She just seems to be slipping away.'

'What does the doctor say?'

'He says she has turned her face to the wall for some reason. I hope it isn't me. I'm so happy with her, and I thought she was happy with me.'

'I'm sure she is,' I said. 'You'd have known very clearly if not, wouldn't you? Mummy's quiet, but she's absolutely no good at dissembling. I'll come down straight away. Today's

Thursday. I'll be there on Saturday morning. Tell her I'm coming, will you? Heavens, I'm so sorry! I never asked your permission!'

'What rubbish!' exclaimed Aunt Bessie. 'You know full well how delighted I will be to see you!'

Although it was June, Mother was in the sitting room wrapped in rugs in front of an open log fire. Aunt Bessie had done wonders with the cottage: there were flowers everywhere, it was as neat as a new pin, and the wooden furniture and the brass door handles sparkled with polish. But because of the fire, the little room was very stuffy.

Mother was in her late eighties now, and she looked it. Her vivid blue eyes were milky, almost blind-looking, and the wispy hair was a white untidy cloud. She was desperately thin, but her smile when she saw me was as radiant as ever. I remembered with a pang of guilt that I had reproved Pippa for calling me Mother, and Bruce, Daddy, yet I had always done the same with my parents. Did that mean that Pippa had inherited her jealousy from me? It seemed so. I went forward and kissed her and she wound her arms round me like a child.

'Oh, darling,' she exclaimed. 'How lovely to see you! How I've missed you! Not that my darling Bessie isn't the best sister in the world. And the nurse who comes in every day is a dear, isn't she, Bessie?' Bessie nodded, looking pleased as Punch. 'But I just wanted to see your sweet little face. I'm feeling a little tired these days.'

'Are you sure I won't tire you more?'

'How could you? You never have.' She laughed the ghost of a laugh. 'How long are you staying?'

'The weekend?'

'Marvellous!' She nodded happily. 'Now sit down and tell me all about yourself, and Bessie will get you a cup of coffee, won't you Bess?'

Bessie hurried out of the room, and I said anxiously, 'It's so

174

good that Aunt Bessie's coming to live here has been such a success, isn't it?'

'The best thing that could have happened to me,' said Mother firmly.

'But she's worried about you, darling. She says you're not eating or sleeping.'

'I sleep so much in little catnaps during the day that there's no sleep left by nightfall. Don't worry about me. I'm fine, but it's time I saw your father again. It's selfish of me, because what will poor Bessie do if I leave her? She is much younger than me, of course, six years, and she's wonderfully fit, you've no idea. But she'll miss me.'

'Don't talk like that, Mother!' I pleaded. 'You sound as if you want to die, and I can't bear it!'

'It's time,' she said again. 'Now, darling,' she went on, 'tell me all *your* news. Everything. What are you doing at the moment?'

'Nothing. But I'm going into a television series quite soon.'

'Good! And Pippa?'

'Not so good. Charles seems to be straying, and Pippa is the last person to cope with a straying husband!'

'Oh dear! The children?'

'As far as I can gather, they seem to be more fond of their father.'

'Oh dear, again! Poor Pippa! Such a difficult child! I hope it all comes right for her! Do you ever see Bruce these days?'

'Indeed I do – he has asked me to marry him again.'

Mother's face lit up. 'Oh, darling, that's the best news of the lot! Your dear father was so fond of Bruce, and so am I! He's a good man, and that's rare. You are going to, aren't you?'

'Yes. In November.'

Her face clouded over. 'So many months away!' she said. 'But my darling, I am so glad! You shouldn't be on your own,

175

and he loves you so much. I never understood why he left you.'

'We're having a honeymoon in the Caribbean,' I said, ignoring her last remark.

'Well! Well! Well!' and she clapped her hands childishly. 'What a very glamorous life you have led, darling! So unlike your father and me! I don't know where you got your talents and looks from, but it's wonderful, and I've always been so proud of you.'

'And I, of both you and Daddy,' I said, firmly, knowing too well that as a child I had often felt ashamed of her both for the chaos of our home, and on parents' day – while being inordinately proud of my handsome father.

She laughed delightedly. 'You're a sweet child,' she said. 'But treasure Bruce now you've got him back, won't you? The older I get, the more I value goodness. It's like a secret excitement when I find the real thing. Sin is always supposed to be such fun, but to me it is unutterably boring. Sin satiates. Real goodness doesn't, and it doesn't cloy, either.'

It was an entirely successful weekend. Mother and I talked about everything under the sun, and I saw once again what my father had loved so much in her; an indomitable spirit, her own sheer goodness, a sharp sense of fun, and complete loyalty. Not a bad combination! I also saw that she had made up her mind to die. She repeated more than once that Bessie would long outlive her, and that the sooner she went the better chance Bessie would have of finding another companion.

As I left her, I felt strangely at peace, knowing how peaceful she herself was.

But Aunt Bessie wasn't. When she said goodbye to me, she spoke fiercely in order to hide the intensity of her unhappiness. Her chin wobbled pathetically, and there were tears in her eyes. In her light linen suit, the man's tie, the heavy boots and the large checked flat cap she wore in summer instead of the battered tweed hat, she looked endearingly comical; but she herself seemed near despair.

'We really get on,' she said. 'You heard her say so, thank God! And it's so good to have a companion again, someone to care for and cook for. It does seem tough luck on a feller that she wants to go. Still, mustn't grumble, I suppose. Something is always better than nothing, and I've enjoyed these last few months. I also like this little place, so that at least is an advantage. Is Pippa coming down to see Josie? If so, I have a feeling she'd better hurry.'

'I'll tell her so,' I said. 'It's so sad. Thank you for all you've done, darling. You've been a brick!'

'Bless you,' said Aunt Bessie gruffly. 'Well, toodle-pip old thing, and carry on with the good work, eh? Oh, and come as often as you can, won't you? She loves you, you know! So do I.'

I promised I would.

I called on Pippa later that evening and found her, as usual, alone.

'Charles is at a meeting,' she said hurriedly. 'He'll be back late.'

'And the children?'

'They're spending a few days with Charles' boss in the country. Isn't that kind of him?'

I looked at her sharply, but she seemed to be quite serious.

'Do they go there often?' I asked.

'They've been twice before and they love it. They both love the horses, and you can't keep horses in London.' She laughed and I forced a smile.

'Don't you ever accompany them?' I was feeling anxious.

'Charles is always there with them – not tonight of course, but nearly always, and there are lots of children round about who are just their own age, so it does them good. Why not stay for a bite of food, Mother? There's plenty in the house, and I can rustle up something in no time!'

I hesitated then said, 'Thank you, darling. I'd love to.'

We talked about my mother for a bit, and Pippa said she'd go and see her at the end of the week. Then I asked about her problems.

'Charles, you mean?'

'Yes, if he's still being a problem.'

'I don't quite know,' she said, 'but it seems to be all right, and he's being very sweet to me. He gave me a diamond bracelet the other day! I don't know what I've done to deserve it. It's really beautiful. I'll show it to you after we've eaten.'

I didn't know what to say: jewellery for the wife, to assuage guilt about having a mistress, is such a hoary old chestnut. I could scarcely believe that Pippa – clever, shrewd, tough little Pippa – had no suspicions.

'Lovely,' I replied weakly. 'I long to see it,' and wondered whether to voice my doubt.

It was a happy evening. For once Pippa seemed completely relaxed with me but, like Agag, I walked delicately.

'I'm really glad you and Daddy are getting married,' she said suddenly.

'Thank you, darling,' I replied, relieved but immediately on my guard. Had Bruce told her already, or was it a ploy to embarrass me – or both of us, perhaps? – for not having told her? I decided to play it straight.

'We're having a honeymoon this time – in the Caribbean!'

'Well! Better late than never,' she replied with a giggle and came over and hugged me.

Perhaps after all we could lay that particular ghost.

CHAPTER TWENTY-THREE

There was a good turn-out for my mother's funeral six weeks later. Everyone was in tears, and Aunt Bessie, in a man's large black felt hat, looked desolate. She had decided to stay on at the little house. Pippa, I was glad to see, was wonderfully kind to her, even asking her up to London for a few days before she started on the next, inevitably lonely, chapter of her life. Aunt Bessie gratefully accepted.

My television work involved rehearsing at Acton, recording in Birmingham, with filming in Shropshire. Bruce's play was still running smoothly at the Duke of York's, and between the two there was little time for us to be together. Relations between Charles and Pippa seemed to remain as they were.

We were married quietly in November; and the night before the wedding I had one of the most extraordinary experiences of my life.

Bruce had finished his packing for the honeymoon and was sitting downstairs in the study. I had just started wondering what clothes to take with me when I decided to try on my wedding suit, which we had had great fun choosing together.

I put it on, and faced the long mirror.

All of a sudden the temperature in the room seemed to drop, and I found myself shivering. In another moment, Philip was in the room with me, standing by my side. He looked the age he had been when we went to South Africa, and very handsome. For some reason it didn't seem strange to me that he was there. He looked into the mirror with me, frowned, shook his head, then pointed angrily at my reflection. I turned to face him. There was no one there – no reflection any longer either. The mirror was empty.

The room became as suddenly warm again as it had been cold, my reflection returned and I felt so ill for a moment or two that I had to sit on the bed. Far back somewhere in my mind, I heard the manic laughter of a ghost in chains.

The whole thing had taken a matter of moments, but I was badly shaken. I thought of calling for Bruce, but didn't want to worry him, so I packed for the honeymoon with shaking hands, and went straight to bed. By the time Bruce came to the bedroom, I was apparently fast asleep. The next morning, I didn't tell him about what had happened.

Our honeymoon in the Caribbean was all that a honeymoon should be, even if we were quite elderly by this time, and it was our second marriage to each other!

First we stayed in Antigua, at the Blue Waters Hotel, which was right on the sea and had a small sandy beach of its own. The sea and sky were a brilliant blue every day of our time there, and it was very hot. There were two large black rocks in the little cove, and from them prehistoric-looking pelicans dived vertically for fish, or stood motionless on the hotel rafts, with hunched shoulders. Until they dived they looked awkward and old, like balding superannuated waiters. In motion they were swift as eagles.

We had left England in a fog, and it had been cold and dismal. We reached Antigua in time for lunch. We swam at once in the warm sea, had Dom Pérignon as an aperitif on the lawn, and lobsters and white wine on the patio for lunch.

The garden was full of hibiscus bushes – crimson, cyclamen-pink, yellow and white. There were roses of every colour, blue plumbago, orange, yellow and red lantanas, scarlet poinsettias, pink oleanders, and crimson and purple bougainvilleas climbing the sides of the hotel. Birds sang, chirped and fluttered in the flame of the forest trees and in the frangipani. Butterflies of a size and hue I'd never seen before – iridescent blue, cream and black, yellow as daffodils, and scarlet and black – were everywhere, and the rough grass was a vivid green.

After a few days we moved on to St Kitts, to the Golden Lemon Hotel – a charming old house with good pictures and excellent food run by a delightful American antique dealer. The beach was speckled in black, as the island was volcanic, but the flowers and the palms and the birds and butterflies rivalled Antigua's, and there were no tourists except the chosen few in the hotel. Every morning a black pig was driven by children to the speckled beach, and with the children bathed ecstatically in the warm sea.

Lastly we went to Nevis, where our hotel was the main house of an old sugar plantation. Here we swam in the hotel pool, or drove a 'mini-moke' down to the mile-long white beach, or walked in the untrammelled countryside, or sunbathed naked and sated in our chalet garden.

It was an idyllic time, but I was haunted by the apparition I had seen on the eve of our wedding. I didn't really believe in ghosts, so I had the choice of either changing my beliefs, or believing that I had, perhaps, imagined the whole thing; conjuring Philip up, as it were, to make my happiness seem a betrayal. As always, he stood between me and my love for Bruce. But this time, thankfully, I preferred my time with Bruce to my dreams of Philip.

I was glad to be back with Bruce; glad to have traded in my independence for the satisfyingly interesting life we had always lived together; glad that he still loved me.

We spent six whole weeks swimming, sunbathing, reading, walking, and catching up with each other about the years between. We heard from Pippa occasionally, but nothing to worry us. Bruce had a few business letters, and I had a letter

181

from the producer of my television series to say that the powers-that-be were very happy with it. We grew close to one another in a way that I hoped would in future be indestructible, and then we made tracks for home.

All was not well with Pippa. With rare sensitivity she had not wanted to interrupt our honeymoon by telling us that Charles had finally left her, taking the two children. He had gone to live with Marcia and he intended to marry her. He couldn't stand his life with Pippa any more, he said. He believed that she had never loved him. He told her that their sex life was unsatisfactory, and he said that their house was more an institution than a home. He said that he'd do the right thing by her, and that she could have unlimited access to the children, whose choice it had been to go with him and Marcia. He said he was sorry, and that he'd like to remain on friendly terms.

Pippa seemed totally bewildered. She had accepted the situation apparently without a struggle, and was living in her house as though it were a fortress. She cried a good deal, and was eating nothing.

'Please come and stay with us, darling,' I said, 'until you've got yourself in hand again. We'd so love to have you, and I want to feed you up a bit.'

'Does Daddy want me?' she asked.

'Of course.'

'Are you sure?'

'Of course.'

'Has he said so?'

'You're our only daughter, darling.'

'I won't come back unless Daddy agrees.'

'If we're going to start all that nonsense again,' I said sharply, 'then I don't want you, either.'

'You misunderstand me, Mummy,' she said quickly ('Mummy', I noticed), 'I've had a lot of time to think things over, and I don't want to be in the way of your happiness. If I come home and Daddy doesn't want me, not only will it make it extremely uncomfortable for all of us, but I may spoil things for you both.'

I kissed her warmly. 'That's kind and thoughtful,' I said. 'Thank you. I'll tell Bruce what you've said, and I have no doubt at all that he'll be as keen as I am that you come home.' I knew that Bruce would prefer to have me to himself, but I also knew that he would not turn her away, any more than I could.

'Home,' she said, and the easy tears were in her eyes again. 'It's the best word in the language, isn't it?'

So she came, and there were the three of us again, all being given a second chance. I remembered Barrie's grim little play, *Dear Brutus*, where all the characters have their second chance and behave exactly as they had done before – but we were luckier. And I must say I admired Pippa – she really tried. She was as loving and gentle to me as she had always been with Bruce, and when I told her how grateful I was, she explained how differently she now felt about us.

'You said once that I had an obsession for Daddy, and I was very angry, I remember, but of course you were right. Luckily for me, when he remarried you, it went. I'd always believed that you were wrong for him, and that one day he would see that to share my life would suit him better. When Mandy left him and he showed no signs of turning towards me, I got a glimmering of the truth, and then when he went back to you I realised that all my life I'd been kidding myself that I was as important to him as he was to me. It was a hell of a shock, I can tell you. But it also brought me to my senses. To him I was only his beloved daughter – nothing more. And very lucky to be his beloved daughter too, I may say.

'I knew then how cruel I had been to you, and I longed to put it right, so this time with you both has been a life-line for me. I don't quite know what I shall do when I leave here, but it'll work out somehow. Charles was right. I wasn't ever in love with him. I married him to show Daddy how attractive I was, and how young he and Mandy and I were compared with you. I enjoyed our marriage for several years, but I suppose Charles finally saw the truth. In a way I'm glad that he's got a chance of real happiness with a woman who is in love with him. He deserves it. As far as the kids are concerned, I'll have to take my chance. My second chance! Perhaps, like being here, things will turn out all right. But I'm going to miss the children.'

'You're much stronger than I am,' I said. 'It took me far longer to grow out of my obsession.'

'Well, so long as you have now,' she said, and grinned.

'Oh yes,' I said. 'That's all passed! And long before Philip shot himself, too. But why leave here? Why not stay on for good? We love having you.'

'Because I've grown up,' she said quietly.

A few days later she said at breakfast, 'I've got myself a job, and I'm quite excited about it.'

Bruce was delighted. 'What sort of job?'

'Lucy Beth Smith – you remember her? – runs a catering firm. They do the meals for VIPs in top businesses. She wants me to go into partnership with her. I've said I'd like to start as one of the cooks first, then if I like what I see, I'll join forces. I'm looking forward to it.'

'When do you begin?' asked Bruce.

'Three weeks today,' said Pippa.

'Good girl!' said Bruce, and he looked at her lovingly. 'Well done!'

'If I *do* do it well,' laughed Pippa, 'congratulate me then!' And it struck me that she was laughing and smiling much more than she used to.

'You will,' said Bruce. 'I know you will.'

She did, and her firm is now expanding fast. She enjoys the work, although the hours are sometimes long. And because she is in with a whole new set of people, she isn't lonely. She is also still remarkably kind to Aunt Bessie, and they have struck up a great friendship (heartwarming for the old girl at her age). Best of all, she is genuinely attracted to one of the VIPs in one of the firms she caters for, and by the sound of it, he is equally attracted to her. She is proceeding cautiously, though, as she's felt a failure ever since Charles left her, and here at least I can help her, as I felt the same when Bruce left me. It is one of the legacies of divorce for the one who is left behind . . .

Families have so much to answer for. They are life-enhancing or life-restricting, the cradle of love or the distorting mirror to adult life. Philip never came to terms with his childhood; Pippa's childhood loves and hates inhibited her adult loving. Childhood can be the only magic left in a world too hard to cope with – it can also be a horror which has to be blasted apart to enable one to live with dignity and success.

Pippa has won through, but in so doing she has abandoned her own children; what will happen to them is another story. She has left us now, and gone back to her house. The three of us are on an even keel. And Bruce and I are happy.

Epilogue

CHAPTER TWENTY-FOUR

One afternoon, June was in her bedroom hanging up a coat she had been wearing for a lunch party, when she heard the front doorbell ring. She went to the head of the stairs, and saw Bruce going down before her.

'I'll get it,' he said. 'Don't worry.'

She went back to the bedroom, and through the open doorway she heard the sound of voices. One was Bruce's. The other – a woman's she didn't recognise. She then heard them going towards the drawing room, so ceased to take an interest: it must be someone for Bruce.

Presently, though, he came to her room, and said tonelessly, 'It's Lady Beverley, darling, and she has come to see you,' and June guessed that for some reason he wasn't pleased.

'Who's Lady Beverley?' she asked.

He sounded impatient. 'Surely you remember? Mary Goodson's sister. The woman Philip went to stay with when Mary died.'

'Of course! What does she want?'

'Apparently to give you some sort of a present,' said Bruce. 'She wouldn't hand it to me. I suppose she wants to talk to you alone.'

June looked at her watch. 'I suppose you wouldn't be an angel, and make us some tea, would you? Then you could join us, and help me get rid of her if she wants to stay too long.'

'OK,' said Bruce grudgingly. 'If that's the way you want it.'

She glanced into the mirror, gave her hair a swift tidy, and followed him downstairs.

Lady Beverley was very tall and very chic. She was as unlike Mary as it was possible to be. Even at this age she was a pretty woman, with blue eyes, beautifully coiffed hair, and lovely legs. She was wearing a fashionable black suit, a small black velvet hat with a veil, and very high heels, and she was standing by the fireplace with her back to the room when June entered. When she saw her, she smiled coolly, and said, 'I'm sorry to intrude like this, but I have only just discovered that I ought to have come to you long ago. My name is Ann Beverley. I'm Mary Goodson's sister.'

'Please sit down,' said June. 'May I take your coat? I've asked my husband Bruce to get us some tea.'

'What an obliging husband!' exclaimed Lady Beverley, sounding amused and supercilious. 'Well trained!' She handed her fur coat to June, and sat in an armchair near the fire, crossing her legs to their best advantage.

'Have you come from Suffolk?' asked June.

'Not today. My husband and I have a house in Eaton Square,' said Lady Beverley. 'We spend most weeks from Mondays to Fridays in London, and the weekends in Suffolk.' She looked around her in apparent satisfaction. 'What a charming house this is! I hadn't heard of Fentiman Street before.' June laughed and she suddenly laughed too. 'That sounded pretty rude, didn't it? I'm so sorry – but it's true, and I like these sort of houses with these large gardens at the foot of those iron steps. It's a good period.'

June nodded agreement. 'You said that you ought to have come to see me some time ago,' she said. 'What do you mean?'

'After poor old Philip died, another of my sisters went to live at Choppins,' said Lady Beverley. 'She's moving now,

190

though – the place is too big for her. She's sold most of the furniture, but I was lucky enough to be given the desk from Philip's bedroom ... a lovely little thing, I have always admired it. Naturally, when I got it home I gave it a thorough inspection, and I found this.'

She opened her large black crocodile handbag and produced a tiny parcel and a letter. She handed them to June.

'The letter is in Philip's handwriting,' she said, 'and it's addressed to you. So is the parcel.'

June took them both. 'Thank you,' she said. 'It's most kind of you to bother.'

'Nonsense. I'm just so sorry you didn't get them before.' She looked at June curiously. 'You knew Philip very well, I understand.'

'Yes.'

'Did you act with him? – I'm sorry, perhaps I should know.'

'I acted with him twice but I met him at drama school. He was one of the tutors,' answered June.

'Ah. That explains it. I thought you were a lot younger.'

'Seventeen years, I believe.'

'Shakespeare says ten years is the right age gap,' said Lady Beverley. 'Orsino and Viola, isn't it? *Twelfth Night?*'

June was surprised, then remembered that Mary had been an actress. 'Were you an actress too?' she asked.

'No, but I've always loved Shakespeare – and my husband is ten years older than me! Aren't you going to open the present? Or is that being too vulgarly curious on my part?'

'If you'll forgive me ...' said June, declining apologetically.

Lady Beverley nodded, smiling wryly. 'Mary was a marvellous wife,' she said. 'Poor Philip! What a childhood! He and Mary were remarkably happy, all things considered,

191

although I think in the end it took more out of Mary than it did out of Philip. Still, she married the man of her dreams, and we don't all do that, do we?'

'No, indeed.'

'The man of her dreams! A very apt description, wouldn't you say? But I can't say that he would have been the man of *my* dreams. Too short. I like my men big and brawny. He was devastatingly attractive to most women, though, I believe. Did you find him attractive?'

'Very.' June was beginning to get restive. 'Most of the girls in my year at school thought so, too.'

'You knew about his father?'

'Yes.'

'Dreadful. Quite dreadful.'

'Yes.'

'The family was very upset when Mary wanted to marry Philip. He wasn't exactly our scene, but we all grew to be very fond of him.'

'I'm glad.'

There was a long pause, then Lady Beverley changed her tone: 'You weren't very good news, I'm afraid.'

June was startled. 'I beg your pardon?' she said.

'We're a very close family, you know.'

'Oh?'

'Mary told me all about you, and how you tried to break up their marriage,' said Lady Beverley, calmly. 'Under the circumstances, a pretty shabby thing to do.'

'I had no idea of the circumstances until I went to see Mary when she was dying,' said June. 'By then it was all over between me and Philip.'

'Not quite,' said Lady Beverley. 'Why do you think he shot himself?'

'Because he couldn't get along without Mary,' said June.

'Your husband had left you by that time, and yet you refused to help Philip.'

192

'I didn't see how I could. Everything was finished between me and Philip long before Mary died.'

'He didn't think so.'

'I telephoned him when Mary died. I also wrote him a letter, which he never answered.'

'You had tried to break up that marriage for years and years, and yet when Mary died and Philip needed you, you made yourself scarce. I'm not a tremendously moral woman, but I do disapprove of what you did.'

'So do I,' agreed June, 'but I couldn't help myself. Philip was an obsession, and where he was concerned I was powerless. I tried. God knows I tried, but it was useless. Then, when I visited Mary and saw how attached he was to *her* – suddenly, it ended. So you see, it was too late, for both of us.'

'You've gone back to your husband now, I gather. He must be a remarkable man. Did you break up because of Philip?'

'We don't really know each other, Lady Beverley,' said June. 'I hope you'll forgive me if I don't answer that question.' She felt uncomfortable and guilty, and slightly outraged.

'I'm unlikely to forgive you,' said Lady Beverley, grimly. 'My little Mary was one of the sweetest women it has ever been my privilege to know. She had a rough time one way and another, and you made things a hundred times worse.'

'Well there's nothing we can do about it now,' said June with some asperity.

'I hope that sometimes you feel ashamed of yourself.'

'I do.'

'And I hope that you are punished for it,' said Lady Beverley.

'I believe I was punished for it throughout the whole affair,' said June. 'I was desperately unhappy most of the time.'

193

'The wages of sin,' said Lady Beverley.

'You have no right to come into a stranger's house and talk like this,' said June angrily.

'When I've gone you'll be glad I did,' replied Lady Beverley imperturbably. 'We all have to cleanse ourselves of our sins, as well as put them behind us. That's what confession is about.'

When Bruce came in with the tea, Lady Beverley's manner changed utterly. She became social, even a little flirtatious, and June could see that Bruce liked her very much.

After she had gone, he said briskly, 'So what was all that about? She's rather fun, isn't she?'

'Not exactly fun,' replied June, and told him most of what had happened.

'So what did Philip give you?' asked Bruce.

June looked across at her husband. His clever, rather heavy face under the thatch of grey hair looked concerned. Still, after all these years, any mention of Philip could disturb him! For him as for June, Philip had been an obsession, and the knowledge wrenched her heart. Bruce was a dominating impatient man by instinct, yet for her sake he had schooled himself to patience. He had taken second place to Philip for years, and even now he feared that he might have to do so again.

She said gently, 'I haven't opened the letter or the parcel, darling, because I've been waiting for you. After all, what can Philip have to say to me now from the other side of the grave?'

'I don't know.'

'Shall I read you the letter?' asked June.

'Don't bother,' said Bruce. 'I'm sure he meant it to be private. Just open the present.'

June did as she was told, and unwrapped a small scarlet leather box. When she opened it, nestling in scarlet velvet was a ruby-and-diamond ring. It was made in an old-fashioned baguette style, but the stones were exceptionally large, and exceptionally beautiful. She gasped. 'My God! It must have cost a bomb!'

'Does it fit?' asked Bruce.

June tried it on the third finger of her right hand and it fitted perfectly.

'Very nice,' said Bruce flatly, and he walked out of the room.

June opened the letter, and read:

My Heart's Darling,

Did you know that I thought of you in those terms, and have done ever since that idiot girl tried to kill me in Chelsea?

At first after the shooting I tried to put you out of my mind, but gradually your image returned to haunt my dreams and settle in my heart. Why this had not happened before, I have no idea – perhaps because it was only when I realised I had lost you, and could take you for granted no longer, that I knew I loved you.

When I did fall, the extraordinary thing was that it didn't affect my love for Mary at all. She was always something different in my life; above and beyond every-thing else. We all have our obsessions. Mary was mine. She was my life's blood, and without her I have no will to live.

Heart's darling! Life's blood! How dramatically I am expressing myself, but then after all I'm an actor, aren't I? Although, alas, not a good one! And that didn't help our affair either, did it?

Tonight I shall kill myself. I have asked that whoever comes across this letter, and the little parcel that goes with it, in this desk in my bedroom, shall give them to you. With my love.

I bought this ring for you the first night of that last play we did together. The last play I did in the West End, as it happens. How excited I was that we were going to be together again! You'll never know how urgently I wanted to effect a reconciliation; to show you how important you were to me! But everything went wrong. It was a complete shambles. A farce. Your feeling for me had gone so completely that you didn't even want to be a friend. I couldn't believe it, and God how I hated those few weeks in that boring unsuccessful run!

I don't know what you feel for me now. It doesn't matter any more. Death will be everlasting peace, I hope, or better still a reuniting with Mary. How lucky I was to find her! My guardian angel. Hell, I'm getting maudlin, but then of course I've had a bit to drink, to steel myself for what I am going to do!

Wear this ring darling, not just in memory of me, but because it is beautiful, and you are beautiful.

Philip

For a long time June sat where she was, the letter open in her hand. So many memories! So much loving – over! But she and Bruce must waste no more time. The present was what counted. The only thing that counted.

She threw the letter into the fire, and watched it burn, the paper waving like a chocolate leaf before it shifted and crumpled into ashes. She put the ring back in the little ring box, and went to her bedroom where she put it at the back of a drawer with other things she never looked at. Then she went to find Bruce.

He was in his study, looking out of the window, where a sudden hurricane of snow was hurling itself out of a steel grey sky at the window panes, and settling, white, on the sills.

'So Philip is back after all,' he said wearily.

'No darling,' said June. 'He's gone ... for both of us.'

Bruce held out his arms, and June walked into them.

196

Philip's voice came into her mind as clearly as though he were speaking out loud. 'Look outward, angel,' he said.

'I will,' answered June, urgently and emphatically.

Bruce looked at her in astonishment.